CLASSIC
SHORT
STORIES

CLASSIC
SHORT
STORIES

CLASSIC
SHORT
STORIES

EDITED BY
PHILIP GARDNER
& NAT NEWMARK

MACMILLAN

First published 1990 by
MACMILLAN EDUCATION AUSTRALIA PTY LTD
107 Moray Street, South Melbourne 3205
Reprinted 1991, 1992, 1993 (twice), 1994 (twice)

Associated companies and representatives
throughout the world.

National Library of Australia
cataloguing in publication data.

Classic short stories.

  ISBN 0 7329 0399 8.

  1. Short stories. I. Gardner, Philip.
  II. Newmark, Nat.

808.831

Typeset by Midland Typesetters, Maryborough, Victoria
Printed in Hong Kong

Illustrated by Betina Ogden
Cover design by Niall Meehan

Contents

Preface

Our aims in producing this anthology were to find short stories that are classics of the genre, and to include the world's most famous short story writers. Given the enormous number of stories available, these are ambitious aims. We could probably make up a list of omitted authors whose stories are just as qualified to be considered "classic", or who are better known as short story writers than some of the authors included in this book. Thus, for example, the works of Somerset Maugham, Saki, O. Henry, Wharton and Hemingway have been omitted. Our decisions are based on a mixture of personal tastes, assessment of literary merit, the likely appeal of particular stories to senior secondary students, as well as a consideration of an author's place in the short story writers' hierarchy.

We have limited the number of stories in the book to fifteen, which we considered to be a reasonable number for students to read and discuss in a unit of study. The stories are presented in alphabetical order, according to the authors' surnames.

As well as the stories themselves, we have included questions, writing activities and notes for each story, and further activities or reading for some stories. This means that the book can be used in different ways, depending on the teacher's or student's purpose. The questions could be used if the intention is to read and show understanding of the stories; the writing activities are intended to help the students to focus on particular elements in the stories, and to emulate these. The further activities take up points that are not central to the stories, but that we found to be interesting. Students may prefer simply to read all the stories and make some general judgements about them. The assignment entitled "General Activities" (see pages 1–4) could be of use for this activity.

Of course, even at senior levels, a skilled reading by the teacher, with the students having a copy of the text in front of them, can heighten both enjoyment and appreciation.

We hope that students find pleasure in reading these stories, and that the activities will help them to develop a critical understanding of what we believe are classic short stories.

General Activities

Review assignment

1 Read at least ten of the stories in this book, then say briefly:
   (a) what happens in each story, and
   (b) what you believe to be the author's purpose. For example: to make the reader laugh or cry; to surprise; to excite; to present a particular idea. It could, of course, be more than one of these. Write approximately fifty words on each story.

2 Select the story that you think best fits each of the following descriptions. In each case, write a paragraph justifying your selection. Include quotations from the story to support your view.

   (a) the story with the most engaging opening (that is, the one that quickly captured your interest)
   (b) the story with the most interesting (unexpected? amusing? infuriating? exciting? clever?) developments in the plot
   (c) the story with the most important or powerful theme
   (d) the story that presents the most interesting or entertaining character(s)
   (e) the story with the most satisfying (amusing? unexpected? thought-provoking?) ending

3 Write a review of the story you most enjoyed. When preparing your review, keep in mind the following points.

   • You will need to give a general account of what the story is about (you could use some of the information you wrote in answer to question 1). However, you should not say too much, or you may destroy your reader's potential pleasure in reading the story. A review should not say what happens at the end of the story; however, you can give information about such things as the general plot, the setting, the writing style, theme, as well as the characters and the way they are developed during the story. You could begin by looking at the title of the story, and talking about what it suggests the story is about.

1

- Give some background information about the author, and place the story in its historical context if you consider this to be helpful. You could use the notes given at the start of the story for this purpose, although further research would be appropriate if, for example, you decide to make comparisons with other stories written by the same author.

- Make sure your attitude towards the story is clear. Presumably you are recommending that someone else read it, and you need to say why you are doing this. Comment on what you consider to be the story's strengths. Did you find it exciting, clever, witty, sad, amusing, touching, enthralling, powerful, interesting, exhilarating, provocative, stimulating, entertaining, poignant?

- Finally, check that your review is clearly and accurately expressed.

4 Write a comparison of two stories that are similar in some way, and say which you prefer. Follow the basic guidelines outlined in question 3. Some possible comparisons are:

- Baynton and Lawson (portrayal of life in the Australian bush)
- Jacobs and Poe (treatment of horror)
- Wells and Thurber (use of humour)
- Chekhov and Tolstoy (portrayal of life in Russia)
- Joyce and Lawrence (relationship between men and women)
- Faulkner and Baynton (use of dialogue).

This list is not complete; there are many other possible points of comparison.

Oral activities

1 Oral review

Prepare the review outlined above, then present it orally to the whole class, or to a smaller group within the class. You could also consider other audiences. For example, you could select a story that you consider to be appropriate for a younger age group, and present your review to such a group. Some points to keep in mind when presenting your review orally are:

- Be prepared to read out appropriate passages to support your points. Look up any words you do not understand or are not sure how to pronounce; practise reading the passage(s) aloud. Your reading should bring out the emotion, excitement, sadness or humour of the story.

• Be aware also of the techniques involved in presenting a talk to an audience, especially:
  —know what you are going to say, and do not read the complete review aloud
  —look at your audience (eye contact is important in communication)
  —speak in a clear, loud voice.
• You may also need to allow some time to answer questions.

2 Reading aloud

Choose one of the short stories and read it aloud to a group. Consider which group is the most appropriate—it may not be your class group, perhaps not even a school group. Some possible groups are:

• your class
• a small group within your class
• another class, perhaps at a different year level
• a group of people on a camp or at a concert
• a community group—perhaps a group of older people who would appreciate the story as entertainment.

When preparing for this activity, some questions you will need to ask yourself are:

• What type of story is most appropriate for my skills? (Some stories are more exciting than others; some contain a greater amount of dialogue; some rely on humour. Each of these requires slightly different reading skills.)

• What changes in pace, volume or pitch are necessary in the reading? (Sad passages may need to be read slowly, relatively softly, and with the voice pitched low; more exciting passages may need to be faster, louder, higher pitched.)

• Are there any words that you do not understand, or that you find difficult to pronounce?

• Do you want your audience to have a copy of the story? (This will depend to some extent on the audience you are reading to—it may be helpful to junior students if they follow your reading of the story; but for a reading at a concert it would be both inappropriate and impractical to supply a copy of the story.)

• If your audience is watching you, what facial expressions and body movements are appropriate to reflect the sadness, humour or tension of the story?

Another way of presenting a story could be a group reading of it. There are a number of stories in this book that could be used for this purpose. For example, "The Malefactor" could be read by two people (Denis and the magistrate); "The Advice" by three people (Monsieur Mestre, the young man and a narrator).

Essay topics

Write an essay on one of the following topics. In your essay, make reference to two or three of the stories in this book.

1 "Short stories are popular because they offer the reader light entertainment and little more."
   Do you agree?

2 "The short story, despite its limitations, has great power and variety."
   (A.L. Clayfield)
   Discuss.

3 "The short story cannot develop characters or ideas, and the interest therefore tends to focus on a tricky plot or surprise ending."
   Do you agree?

4 "Despite its relative brevity, the short story is still able to capture our minds and emotions—it can make us think and it can make us feel."
   Discuss.

5 Read the definition of a short story given by Edgar Allan Poe (see page 96), then use it to discuss the features of two or more of the stories in this book.

6 Select two or three of the stories that had an impact on you and discuss them in some detail. Your discussion may include such features as theme, subject matter (briefly), setting, character, type of story, any distinctive qualities and the overall effectiveness of each story.

Barbara Baynton
Squeaker's Mate

Barbara Baynton (1857-1929) was born Barbara Lawrence in Scone, NSW. She married a selector, Alexander Frater, in 1880. She divorced him for desertion in 1890, then married Thomas Baynton, a retired surgeon of Sydney, in the same year. It was then that she began writing, her first published story appearing in the *Bulletin* in 1896.

This story is from her collection *Bush Studies* (1902), published in England. After her second husband's death in 1904 she divided her time between England and Australia. In 1921 she married Lord Headley.

Barbara Baynton's stories are a grim contrast to the romantic view of bush life expressed by most of her contemporaries.

THE woman carried the bag with the axe and maul and wedges; the man had the billy and clean tucker-bags; the cross-cut saw linked them. She was taller than the man, and the equability of her body, contrasting with his indolent slouch, accentuated the difference. "Squeaker's mate", the men called her, and these agreed that she was the best long-haired mate that ever stepped in petticoats. The selectors' wives pretended to challenge her right to womanly garments, but if she knew what they said, it neither turned nor troubled Squeaker's mate.

Nine prospective posts and maybe sixteen rails—she calculated this yellow gum would yield. "Come on," she encouraged the man; "let's tackle it."

From the bag she took the axe, and ring-barked a preparatory circle, while he looked for a shady spot for the billy and tucker-bags.

"Come on." She was waiting with the greased saw. He came. The saw rasped through a few inches, then he stopped and looked at the sun.

"It's nigh tucker-time," he said, and when she dissented, he exclaimed, with sudden energy, "There's another bee! Wait, you go on with the axe, an' I'll track 'im."

As they came, they had already followed one and located the nest.

5

She could not see the bee he spoke of, though her grey eyes were as keen as a black's. However, she knew the man, and her tolerance was of the mysteries.

She drew out the saw, spat on her hands, and with the axe began weakening the inclining side of the tree.

Long and steadily and in secret the worm had been busy in the heart. Suddenly the axe blade sank softly, the tree's wounded edges closed on it like a vice. There was a "settling" quiver on its top branches, which the woman heard and understood. The man, encouraged by the sounds of the axe, had returned with an armful of sticks for the billy. he shouted gleefully, "It's fallin', look out."

But she waited to free the axe.

With a shivering groan the tree fell, and as she sprang aside, a thick worm-eaten branch snapped at a joint and silently she went down under it.

"I tole yer t' look out," he reminded her, as with a crow-bar, and grunting earnestly, he forced it up. "Now get out quick."

She tried moving her arms and the upper part of her body. Do this; do that, he directed, but she made no movement after the first.

He was impatient, because for once he had actually to use his strength. His share of a heavy lift usually consisted of a make-believe grunt, delivered at a critical moment. Yet he hardly cared to let it again fall on her, though he told her he would, if she "didn't shift".

Near him lay a piece broken short; with his foot he drew it nearer, then gradually worked it into a position, till it acted as a stay to the lever.

He laid her on her back when he drew her out, and waited expecting some acknowledgement of his exertions, but she was silent, and as she did not notice that the axe she had tried to save lay with the fallen trunk across it, he told her. She cared almost tenderly for all their possessions and treated them as friends. But the half-buried broken axe did not affect her. He wondered a little, for only last week she had patiently chipped out the old broken head, and put in a new handle.

"Feel bad?" he inquired at length.

"Pipe," she replied with slack lips.

Both pipes lay in the fork of a near tree. He took his, shook out the ashes, filled it, picked up a coal and puffed till it was alight— then he filled hers. Taking a small fire-stick he handed her the pipe. The hand she raised shook and closed in an uncertain hold, but she managed by a great effort to get it to her mouth. He lost patience with the swaying hand that tried to take the light.

"Quick," he said "quick, that damn dog's at the tucker."

He thrust it into her hand that dropped helplessly across her chest.

The lighted stick, falling between her bare arm and the dress, slowly roasted the flesh and smouldered the clothes.

He rescued their dinner, pelted his dog out of sight—hers was lying near her head—put on the billy, then came back to her.

The pipe had fallen from her lips; there was blood on the stem.

"Did yer jam yer tongue?" he asked.

She always ignored trifles, he knew, therefore he passed her silence.

He told her that her dress was on fire. She took no heed. He put it out, and looked at the burnt arm, then with intentness at her.

Her eyes were turned unblinkingly to the heavens, her lips were grimly apart, and a strange greyness was upon her face, and the sweat-beads were mixing.

"Like a drink er tea? Asleep?"

He broke a green branch from the fallen tree and swished from his face the multitudes of flies that had descended with it.

In a heavy way he wondered why did she sweat, when she was not working? Why did she not keep the flies out of her mouth and eyes? She'd have bungy eyes, if she didn't. If she was asleep, why did she not close them?

But asleep or awake, as the billy began to boil, he left her, made the tea, and ate his dinner. His dog had disappeared, and as it did not come to his whistle, he threw the pieces to hers, that would not leave her head to reach them.

He whistled tunelessly his one air, beating his own time with a stick on the toe of his blucher, then looked overhead at the sun and calculated that she must have been lying like that for "close up an hour". He noticed that the axe handle was broken in two places, and speculated a little as to whether she would again pick out the back-broken handle or burn it out in his method, which was less trouble, if it did spoil the temper of the blade. He examined the worm-dust in the stump and limbs of the newly fallen tree; mounted it and looked round the plain. The sheep were straggling in a manner that meant walking work to round them, and he supposed he would have to yard them tonight, if she didn't liven up. He looked down at unenlivened her. This changed his "chune" to a call for his hiding dog.

"Come on, ole feller," he commanded her dog. "Fetch 'em back." He whistled further instructions, slapping his thigh and pointing to the sheep.

But a brace of wrinkles either side of the brute's closed mouth demonstrated determined disobedience. The dog would go if she told him, and by and by she would.

He lighted his pipe and killed half an hour smoking. With the frugality that hard graft begets, his mate limited both his and her own tobacco, so he must not smoke all afternoon. There was no work to shirk, so time began to drag. Then a "goanner" crawling up a tree attracted him. He gathered various missiles and tried vainly to hit the seemingly grinning reptile. He came back and sneaked a fill of her tobacco, and while he was smoking, the white tilt of a cart caught his eye. He jumped up. "There's Red Bob goin' t'our place fur th' 'oney," he said. "I'll go an' weigh it an' get the gonz" (money).

He ran for the cart, and kept looking back as if fearing she would follow and thwart him.

Red Bob the dealer was, in a business way, greatly concerned, when he found that Squeaker's mate was "'avin' a sleep out there 'cos a tree fell on her". She was the best honey-strainer and boiler that he dealt with. She was straight and square too. There was no water in her honey whether boiled or merely strained, and in every kerosene-tin the weight of honey was to an ounce as she said. Besides he was suspicious and diffident of paying the indecently eager Squeaker before he saw the woman. So reluctantly Squeaker led to where she lay. With many fierce oaths Red Bob sent her lawful protector for help, and compassionately poured a little from his flask down her throat, then swished away the flies from her till help came.

Together these men stripped a sheet of bark, and laying her with pathetic tenderness upon it, carried her to her hut. Squeaker followed in the rear with the billy and tucker.

Red Bob took his horse from the cart, and went to town for the doctor. Late that night at the back of the old hut (there were two) he and others who had heard that she was hurt, squatted with unlighted pipes in their mouths, waiting to hear the doctor's verdict. After he had given it and gone, they discussed in whispers, and with a look seen only on bush faces, the hard luck of that woman who alone had hard-grafted with the best of them for every acre and hoof on that selection. Squeaker would go through it in no time. Why she had allowed it to be taken up in his name, when the money had been her own, was also for them among the mysteries.

Him they called "a nole woman", not because he was hanging round the honey-tins, but after man's fashion to eliminate all virtue. They beckoned him, and explaining his mate's injury, cautioned him to keep from her the knowledge that she would be for ever a cripple.

"Jus' th' same, now, then fur 'im," pointing to Red Bob, "t' pay me, I'll 'ev t' go t' town."

They told him in whispers what they thought of him, and with a cowardly look towards where she lay, but without a word of parting, like shadows these men made for their homes.

Next day the women came. Squeaker's mate was not a favourite with them—a woman with no leisure for yarning was not likely to be. After the first day they left her severely alone, their plea to their husbands, her uncompromising independence. It is in the ordering of things that by degrees most husbands accept their wives' views of other women.

The flour bespattering Squeaker's now neglected clothes spoke eloquently of his clumsy efforts at damper making. The women gave him many a feed, agreeing that it must be miserable for him.

If it were miserable and lonely for his mate, she did not complain; for her the long, long days would give place to longer nights—those nights with the pregnant bush silence suddenly cleft by a bush voice. However, she was not fanciful, and being a bush scholar knew 'twas a dingo, when a long whine came from the scrub on the skirts of which lay the axe under the worm-eaten tree. That quivering wail from the billabong lying murkily mystic towards the East was only the cry of the fearing curlew.

Always her dog—wakeful and watchful as she—patiently waiting for her to be up and about again. That would be soon, she told her complaining mate.

"Yer won't. Yer back's broke," said Squeaker laconically. "That's wot's wrong er yer; injoory t' th' spine. Doctor says that means back's broke, and yer won't never walk no more. No good not t' tell yer, cos I can't be doin' everythin'."

A wild look grew on her face, and she tried to sit up.

"Erh," said he, "see! yer carnt, yer jes' ther same as a snake w'en ees back's broke, on'y yer don't bite yerself like a snake does w'en 'e carnt crawl. Yer did bite yer tongue w'en yer fell."

She gasped, and he could hear her heart beating when she let her head fall back a few moments; though she wiped her wet forehead with the back of her hand, and still said that was the doctor's mistake. But day after day she tested her strength, and whatever the result, was silent, though white witnesses, halo-wise, gradually circled her brow and temples.

"'Tisn't as if yer was agoin' t' get better t'morrer, the doctor says yer won't never work no more, an' I can't be cookin' an' workin' an' doin' everythin'!"

He muttered something about "sellin' out", but she firmly refused to think of such a monstrous proposal.

He went into town one Saturday afternoon soon after, and did not return till Monday.

Her supplies, a billy of tea and scraps of salt beef and damper (her dog got the beef), gave out the first day, though that was as nothing to her compared with the bleat of the penned sheep, for it was summer and droughty, and her dog could not unpen them.

Of them and her dog only she spoke when he returned. He d—d him, and d—d her, and told her to "double up yer ole broke back an' bite yerself". He threw things about, made a long-range feint of kicking her threatening dog, then sat outside in the shade of the old hut, nursing his head till he slept.

She, for many reasons, had when necessary made these trips into town, walking both ways, leading a pack-horse for supplies. She never failed to indulge him in a half pint—a pipe was her luxury.

The sheep waited till next day, so did she.

For a few days he worked a little in her sight; not much—he never did. It was she who always lifted the heavy end of the log, and carried the tools; he—the billy and tucker.

She wearily watched him idling his time; reminded him that the wire lying near the fence would rust, one could run the wire through easily, and when she got up in a day or so, she would help strain and fasten it. At first he pretended he had done it, later said he wasn't goin' t' go wirin' or nothin' else by 'imself if every other man on the place did.

She spoke of many other things that could be done by one, reserving the great till she was well. Sometimes he whistled while she spoke, often swore, generally went out, and when this was inconvenient, dull as he was, he found the "Go and bite yerself like a snake", would instantly silence her.

At last the work worry ceased to exercise her, and for night to bring him home was a rare thing.

Her dog rounded and yarded the sheep when the sun went down and there was no sign of him, and together they kept watch on their movements till dawn. She was mindful not to speak of this care to him, knowing he would have left it for them to do constantly, and she noticed that what little interest he seemed to share went to the sheep. Why, was soon demonstrated.

Through the cracks her ever watchful eyes one day saw the dust rise out of the plain. Nearer it came till she saw him and a man on horseback rounding and driving the sheep into the yard, and later both left in charge of a little mob. Their "Baa-baas" to her were cries for help; many had been pets. So he was selling her sheep to the town butchers.

In the middle of the next week he came from town with a fresh horse, new saddle and bridle. He wore a flash red shirt, and round his neck a silk handkerchief. On the next occasion she smelt scent, and though he did not try to display the dandy meerschaum, she saw it, and heard the squeak of the new boots, not bluchers. However he was kinder to her this time, offering a fill of his cut tobacco; he had

long ceased to keep her supplied. Several of the men who sometimes in passing took a look in, would have made up her loss had they known, but no word of complaint passed her lips.

She looked at Squeaker as he filled his pipe from his pouch, but he would not meet her eyes, and, seemingly dreading something, slipped out.

She heard him hammering in the old hut at the back, which served for tools and other things which sunlight and rain did not hurt. Quite briskly he went in and out. She could see him through the cracks carrying a narrow strip of bark, and understood, he was making a bunk. When it was finished he had a smoke, then came to her and fidgetted about; he said this hut was too cold and that she would never get well in it. She did not feel cold, but, submitting to his mood, allowed him to make a fire that would roast a sheep. He took off his hat, and, fanning himself, said he was roastin', wasn't she? She was.

He offered to carry her into the other; he would put a new roof on it in a day or two, and it would be better than this one, and she would be up in no time. He stood to say this where she could not see him.

His eagerness had tripped him.

There were months to run before all the Government conditions of residence, etc., in connection with the selection, would be fulfilled, still she thought perhaps he was trying to sell out, and she would not go.

He was away four days that time, and when he returned slept in the new bunk.

She compromised. Would he put a bunk there for himself, keep out of town, and not sell the place? He promised instantly with additions.

"Try could yer crawl yerself?" he coaxed, looking at her bulk.

Her nostrils quivered with her suppressed breathing, and her lips tightened, but she did not attempt to move.

It was evident some great purpose actuated him. After attempts to carry and drag her, he rolled her on the sheet of bark that had brought her home, and laboriously drew her round.

She asked for a drink, he placed her billy and tin pint beside the bunk, and left her, gasping and dazed, to her sympathetic dog.

She saw him run up and yard his horse, and though she called him, he would not answer nor come.

When he rode swiftly towards the town, her dog leaped on the bunk, and joined a refrain to her lamentation, but the cat took to the bush.

He came back at dusk next day in a spring cart—not alone—he had another mate. She saw her though he came a roundabout way, trying to keep in front of the new hut.

There were noises of moving many things from the cart to the hut. Finally he came to a crack near where she lay, and whispered the promise of many good things to her if she kept quiet, and that he would set her hut afire if she didn't. She was quiet, he need not have feared, for that time she was past it, she was stunned.

The released horse came stumbling round to the old hut, and thrust its head in the door in a domesticated fashion. Her dog promptly resented this straggler mistaking their hut for a stable. And the dog's angry dissent, together with the shod clatter of the rapidly disappearing intruder, seemed to have a disturbing effect on the pair in the new hut. The settling sounds suddenly ceased, and the cripple heard the stranger close the door, despite Squeaker's assurances that the woman in the old hut could not move from her bunk to save her life, and that her dog would not leave her.

Food, more and better, was placed near her—but, dumb and motionless, she lay with her face turned to the wall, and her dog growled menacingly at the stranger. The new woman was uneasy, and told Squeaker what people might say and do if she died.

He, scared at the "do", went into the bush and waited.

She went to the door, not the crack, the face was turned that way, and said she had come to cook and take care of her

The disabled woman, turning her head slowly, looked steadily at her. She was not much to look at. Her red hair hung in an uncurled bang over her forehead, the lower part of her face had robbed the upper, and her figure evinced imminent motherhood, though it is doubtful if the barren woman, noting this, knew by calculation the paternity was not Squeaker's. She was not learned in these matters, though she understood all about an ewe and lamb.

One circumstance was apparent—ah! bitterest of all bitterness to women—she was younger.

The thick hair that fell from the brow of the woman on the bunk was white now.

Bread and butter the woman brought. The cripple looked at it, at her dog, at the woman. Bread and butter for a dog! but the stranger did not understand till she saw it offered to the dog. The bread and butter was not for the dog. She brought meat.

All next day the man kept hidden. The cripple saw his dog, and knew he was about.

But there was an end of this pretence when at dusk he came back with a show of haste, and a finger of his right hand bound and ostentatiously prominent. His entrance caused great excitement to his new mate. The old mate, who knew this snake-bite trick from its inception, maybe, realised how useless were the terrified stranger's

13

efforts to rouse the snoring man after an empty pint bottle had been flung on the outside heap.

However, what the sick woman thought was not definite, for she kept silent always. Neither was it clear how much she ate, and how much she gave to her dog, though the new mate said to Squeaker one day that she believed that the dog would not take a bite more than its share.

The cripple's silence told on the stranger, especially when alone. She would rather have abuse. Eagerly she counted the days past and to pass. Then back to the town. She told no word of that hope to Squeaker, he had no place in her plans for the future. So if he spoke of what they would do by and by when his time would be up, and he able to sell out, she listened in uninterested silence.

She did tell him she was afraid of "her", and after the first day would not go within reach, but every morning made a billy of tea, which with bread and beef Squeaker carried to her.

The rubbish heap was adorned, for the first time, with jam and fish tins from the table in the new hut. It seemed to be understood that neither woman nor dog in the old hut required them.

Squeaker's dog sniffed and barked joyfully around them till his licking efforts to bottom a salmon tin sent him careering in a muzzled frenzy, that caused the younger woman's thick lips to part grinningly till he came too close.

The remaining sheep were regularly yarded. His old mate heard him whistle as he did it. Squeaker began to work about a little burning-off. So that now, added to the other bush voices, was the call from some untimely falling giant. There is no sound so human as that from the riven souls of these tree people, or the trembling sighs of their upright neighbours whose hands in time will meet over the victim's fallen body.

There was no bunk on the side of the hut to which her eyes turned, but her dog filled that space, and the flash that passed between this back-broken woman and her dog might have been the spirit of these slain tree folk, it was so wondrous ghostly. Still, at times, the practical in her would be dominant, for in a mind so free of fancies, backed by bodily strength, hope died slowly, and forgetful of self she would almost call to Squeaker her fears that certain bees' nests were in danger.

He went into town one day and returned, as he had promised, long before sundown, and next day a clothes-line bridged the space between two trees near the back of the old hut; and—an equally rare occurrence— Squeaker placed across his shoulders the yoke that his old mate had fashioned for herself, with two kerosene-tins attached, and brought them filled with water from the distant creek; but both only partly filled the tub, a new purchase. With utter disregard of the heat and Squeaker's sweating brow, his new mate said, even after another trip, two more now for the blue water. Under her commands he brought them, though sullenly, perhaps contrasting the old mate's methods with the new.

His old mate had periodically carried their washing to the creek, and his moleskins had been as white as snow without aid of blue.

Towards noon, on the clothes-line many strange garments fluttered, suggestive of a taunt to the barren woman. When the sun went down she could have seen the assiduous Squeaker lower the new prop-sticks and considerately stoop to gather the pegs his inconsiderate new mate had dropped. However, after one load of water next morning, on hearing her estimate that three more would put her own things through, Squeaker struck. Nothing he could urge would induce the stranger to trudge to the creek, where thirst-slaked snakes lay waiting for someone to bite. She sulked and pretended to pack up, till a bright idea struck Squeaker. He fastened a cask on a sledge and, harnessing the new horse, hitched him to it, and, under the approving eyes of his new mate, led off to the creek, though, when she went inside, he bestrode the spiritless brute.

He had various mishaps, any one of which would have served as an excuse to his old mate, but even babes soon know on whom to impose. With an energy new to him he persevered and filled the cask, but the old horse repudiated such a burden even under Squeaker's unmerciful welts. Almost half was sorrowfully baled out, and under a rain of whacks the horse shifted it a few paces, but the cask tilted and the thirsty earth got its contents. All Squeaker's adjectives over his wasted labour were as unavailing as the cure for spilt milk.

It took skill and patience to rig the cask again. He partly filled it, and, just as success seemed probable, the rusty wire fastening the cask to the sledge snapped with the strain, and, springing free, coiled affectionately round the terrified horse's hocks. Despite the sledge (the cask had been soon disposed of) that old town horse's pace then was his record. Hours after, on the plain that met the horizon, loomed two specks: the distance between them might be gauged, for the larger was Squeaker.

Anticipating a plentiful supply and lacking in bush caution, the new mate used the half-bucket of water to boil the salt mutton. Towards noon she laid this joint and bread on the rough table, then watched anxiously in the wrong direction for Squeaker.

She had drained the new tea-pot earlier, but she placed the spout to her thirsty mouth again.

She continued looking for him for hours.

Had he sneaked off to town, thinking she had not used that water, or not caring whether or no? She did not trust him; another had left her. Besides she judged Squeaker by his treatment of the woman who was lying in there with wide-open eyes. Anyhow no use to cry with only that silent woman to hear her.

Had she drunk all hers?

She tried to see at long range through the cracks, but the hanging bed-clothes hid the billy. She went to the door, and, avoiding the bunk looked at the billy.

It was half full.

Instinctively she knew that the eyes of the woman were upon her. She turned away, and hoped and waited for thirsty minutes that seemed hours.

Desperation drove her back to the door. Dared she? No, she couldn't.

Getting a long forked prop-stick, she tried to reach it from the door, but the dog sprang at the stick. She dropped it and ran.

A scraggy growth fringed the edge of the plain. There was the creek. How far? she wondered. Oh, very far, she knew, and besides there were only a few holes where water was, and the snakes; for Squeaker, with a desire to shine in her eyes, was continually telling her of snakes— vicious and many—that daily he did battle with.

She recalled the evening he came from hiding in the scrub with a string around one finger, and said a snake had bitten him. He had drunk the pint of brandy she had brought for her sickness, and then slept till morning. True, although next day he had to dig for the string round the blue swollen finger, he was not worse than the many she had seen at the Shearer's Rest suffering a recovery. There was no brandy to cure her if she were bitten.

She cried a little in self-pity, then withdrew her eyes, that were getting red, from the outlying creek, and went again to the door. She of the bunk lay with closed eyes.

Was she asleep? The stranger's heart leapt, yet she was hardly in earnest as she tip-toed billy-wards. The dog, crouching with head between two paws, eyed her steadily, but showed no opposition. She made dumb show. "I want to be friends with you, and won't hurt her." Abruptly she looked at her, then at the dog. He was motionless and emotionless. Besides if that dog—certainly watching her—wanted to bite her (her dry mouth opened) it could get her any time.

She rated this dog's intelligence almost human, from many of its actions in omission and commission in connection with this woman.

She regretted the pole, no dog would stand that.

Two more steps.

Now just one more; then, by bending and stretching her arm, she would reach it. Could she now? She tried to encourage herself by remembering how close on the first day she had been to the woman, and how delicious a few mouthfuls would be—swallowing dry mouthfuls.

She measured the space between where she had first stood and the billy. Could she get anything to draw it to her? No, the dog would not stand that, and besides the handle would rattle, and she might hear and open her eyes.

The thought of those sunken eyes suddenly opening made her heart bound. Oh! she must breathe—deep, loud breaths. Her throat clicked noisily. Looking back fearfully, she went swiftly out.

She did not look for Squeaker this time, she had given him up.

While she waited for her breath to steady, to her relief and surprise the dog came out. She made a rush to the new hut, but he passed seemingly oblivious of her, and, bounding across the plain, began rounding the sheep. Then he must know Squeaker had gone to town.

Stay! Her heart beat violently; was it because she on the bunk slept and did not want him?

She waited till her heart quieted, and again crept to the door.

The head of the woman on the bunk had fallen towards the wall as in deep sleep; it was turned from the billy, to which she must creep so softly.

Slower, from caution and deadly earnestness, she entered.

She was not so advanced as before, and felt fairly secure, for the woman's eyes were still turned to the wall, and so tightly closed she could not possibly see where she was.

She would bend right down, and try and reach it from where she was.

She bent.

It was so swift and sudden, that she had not time to scream when those bony fingers had gripped the hand that she prematurely reached for the billy. She was frozen with horror for a moment, then her screams were piercing. Panting with victory, the prostrate one held her with a hold that the other did not attempt to free herself from.

Down, down she drew her.

Her lips had drawn back from her teeth, and her breath almost scorched the face that she held so close for the staring eyes to gloat over. Her exultation was so great that she could only gloat and gasp, and hold with a tension that had stopped the victim's circulation.

As a wounded, robbed tigress might hold and look, she held and looked.

Neither heard the swift steps of the man, and if the tigress saw him enter, she was not daunted. "Take me from her," shrieked the terrified one. "Quick, take me from her," she repeated it again, nothing else.

"Take me from her."

He hastily fastened the door and said something that the shrieks drowned, then picked up the pole. It fell with a thud across the arms which the tightening sinews had turned into steel. Once, twice, thrice. Then the one that got the fullest force bent; that side of the victim was free.

The pole had snapped. Another blow with a broken end freed the other side.

Still shrieking "Take me from her, take me from her," she beat on the closed door till Squeaker opened it.

Then he had to face and reckon with his old mate's maddened dog, that the closed door had baffled.

The dog suffered the shrieking woman to pass, but though Squeaker, in bitten agony, broke the stick across the dog, he was forced to give the savage brute best.

"Call 'im orf, Mary, 'e's eatin' me," he implored. "Oh, corl 'im orf."

But with stony face the woman lay motionless.

"Sool 'im on t' 'er." He indicated his new mate who, as though all the plain led to the desired town, still ran in unreasoning terror.

"It's orl 'er doin'," he pleaded, springing on the bunk beside his old mate. But when, to rouse her sympathy, he would have laid his hand on her, the dog's teeth fastened in it and pulled him back.

❖

Questions

1 What do we find out about the characters in the first paragraphs of the story?
2 (a) What indications are given on page 6 that the accident is serious?
  (b) At this stage, what indications are there that Squeaker does not realise what has happened?
  (Refer to specific sentences to justify your answer.)
3 Find examples which show that Squeaker is insensitive to his wife's predicament.
4 Squeaker asks himself a series of questions (page 7) but seems unable to answer them. He wondered "in a heavy way" why she was behaving as she was. What does the word "heavy" suggest about Squeaker?
5 Explain the meaning of the following quotations:
  (a) *But a brace of wrinkles either side the brute's closed mouth demonstrated determined disobedience.* (page 7)

(b) *With the frugality that hard graft begets*... (page 7)

(c) *He, scared at the "do"*... (page 13). It will help if you re-read the previous paragraph before you answer.

(d) *She regretted the pole, no dog would stand that.* (page 16)

6 Look at the paragraph that begins with the sentence: "Next day the women came." (pages 8–9)

  (a) What does this paragraph suggest about the role of women in Australian society at the time?

  (b) How do you think women today would react in the same circumstances?

7 Write three general statements that comment on the character of Squeaker. Find a quotation that substantiates each of your general statements.

For example:

Statement: Squeaker is lazy.

Evidence: *At first he pretended he had done it, later said he wasn't goin' t' go wirin' or nothin' else by 'imself if every other man on the place did.* (page 10)

8 In what ways does Squeaker's mate's dog demonstrate loyalty to her?

Writing

Write a story of betrayal and loyalty. You could use some of the techniques used by Baynton. For example:

• Characters are described in an understated way. The author tells us what the characters do and say rather than commenting directly. It is left to the reader to make judgements about the characters.

• On page 17, a number of short paragraphs are used, suggestive of a shooting script for a film. This speeds up the action. Use a similar technique in your story.

• The loyalty of the dog to Squeaker's mate is juxtaposed with the disloyalty of Squeaker. In your story, include a character that is loyal and one that is disloyal.

Notes

page 5 *maul:* a type of heavy hammer used for driving wedges into logs in order to split them.

  posts and rails: used for making fences (the rails are the horizontal supports).

page 6 *her tolerance was of the mysteries:* mysteries are religious truths that are divinely revealed but remain beyond human comprehension—it is extraordinary that Squeaker's wife should be so tolerant of him.

page 7 *blucher:* calf-length boots, named after Marshal Blucher, head of the Prussian forces at the battle of Waterloo. Note that they are referred to again on page 10 *(. . . and heard the squeak of the new boots, not bluchers).* These boots would have been ankle length and considered to be dressier or more fashionable than bluchers.

page 8 *kerosene-tin:* these 4-gallon (approximately 24-litre) tins were very important in the bush because they were used as buckets, as general containers, or even as drawers in bush cupboards.
selection: a piece of land granted by the government. One of the conditions was that the recipient should build a dwelling and reside in it for a specified time (see also page 12).

page 9 *bush scholar:* she was not a very accurate observer of bush birds! The call of the curlew could not be described as a "quivering wail". The "fearing curlew" is more likely to have been a sandpiper, or a lapwing, both common on the inland plains where this story is set.
bite yourself like a snake: the action of a mortally wounded snake—an involuntary twitching when its back is broken.

page 10 *meerschaum:* type of tobacco pipe named after the clay-like substance used to make the bowl.

page 13 *snake-bite trick:* brandy was believed to be a cure for snake bite. Squeaker is pretending to have been bitten by a snake to justify his drinking.

page 15 *blue water/blue:* blue (made by the soap company Reckitts) was a cleaning product that added a slight blue colour to clothes, making them seem whiter and cleaner.
prop-stick: a forked stick that was used to raise the clothes line high enough to enable it to catch a greater amount of drying wind; or simply to make sure that the heavy, wet washing would not touch the ground.

Anton Chekhov
The Malefactor

The grandson of a serf, Anton Chekhov (1860-1904) was born in
Taganrog, which is in southern Russia. On completion of his medical
studies he pursued a literary career. He became known first through
his short stories, but his plays such as *The Seagull* and *The Cherry
Orchard* are his greatest achievements.

This story is an early one. It revolves around a peasant and a magistrate
failing to understand each other. The magistrate sees the peasant as
a "malefactor"—a criminal or evil-doer. It is illustrative of Chekhov's
persistent preoccupations: human weakness and failure to
communicate.

BEFORE the examining magistrate stands a short, extremely skinny
little peasant wearing a shirt made of ticking and baggy trousers
covered in patches. His face, which is overgrown with hair and pitted
with pock-marks, and his eyes, which are barely visible beneath their
heavy, beetling brows, wear a grim, sullen expression. He has a whole
shock of tangled hair that has not seen a comb for ages, and this lends
him an even greater, spider-like grimness. He is barefoot.

"Denis Grigoryev!" the magistrate begins. "Stand closer and answer
my questions. On July 7th of this year Ivan Semyonov Akinfov, the
railway watchman, was making his morning inspection of the track,
when he came across you at verst 141 unscrewing one of the nuts
with which the rails are secured to the sleepers. This nut, to be precise!
. . . And he detained you with the said nut in your possession. Is that
correct?"

"Wossat?"

"Did all this happen as Akinfov has stated?"

"Course it did."

"Right. So why were you unscrewing the nut?"

"Wossat?"

"Stop saying 'Wossat?' to everything, and answer my question: why
were you unscrewing this nut?"

"Wouldn't have been unscrewing it if I hadn't needed it, would I?" croaks Denis, squinting at the ceiling.

"And why did you need it?"

"What, that nut? We make sinkers out of them nuts . . . "

"Who do you mean—'we'?"

"Us folks . . . Us Klimovo peasants, I mean."

"Listen here, my friend, stop pretending you're an idiot and talk some sense. I don't want any lies about sinkers, do you hear?"

"Lies? I never told a lie in my life . . . " mutters Denis, blinking. "We got to have sinkers, haven't we, your honour? If you put a live-bait or a worm on, he won't sink without a weight, will he? Hah, 'lies' . . . " Denis sniggers. "Ain't no use in a live-bait that floats on the top! Your perch, your pike and your burbot always go for a bait on the bottom. Only a spockerel takes one that's floating on top, and not always then . . . There aren't no spockerel in our rivers . . . He likes the open more, does that one."

"Why are you telling me about spockerels?"

"Wossat? You asked me, that's why! The gents round here fish that way, too. Even a little nipper wouldn't try catching fish without a sinker. 'Course, those as don't understand anything about it, they might. Fools are a law unto 'mselves . . . "

"So you are saying you unscrewed this nut in order to make a sinker out of it?"

"What else for? Not for playing fivestones with!"

"But you could have used some lead for a sinker, a piece of shot . . . or a nail . . . "

"You don't find lead on the railway, you got to buy it, and a nail's no good. You won't find anything better than a nut . . . It's heavy, and it's got a hole through it."

"Stop pretending you're daft, as though you were born yesterday or fell off the moon! Don't you understand, you blockhead, what unscrewing these nuts leads to? If the watchman hadn't been keeping a look-out, a train could have been derailed, people could have been killed! You would have killed people!"

"Lord forbid, your honour! What would I want to kill people for? Do you take us for heathens or some kind of robbers? Glory be, sir, in all our born days we've never so much as thought of doing such things, let alone killed anyone . . . Holy Mother of Heaven save us, have mercy on us . . . What a thing to say!"

"Why do you think train crashes happen, then? Unscrew two or three of these nuts, and you've got a crash!"

Denis sniggers, and peers at the magistrate sceptically.

"Hah! All these years our village's been unscrewing these nuts and the Lord's preserved us, and here you go talking about crashes—me killing people . . . Now if I'd taken a rail out, say, or put a log across that there track, then I grant you that'd brought the train off, but a little nut? Hah!"

"But don't you understand, it's the nuts and bolts that hold the rails to the sleepers!"

"We do understand . . . We don't screw them all off . . . we leave some . . . We're not stupid—we know what we're doing . . . "

Denis yawns and make the sign of the cross over his mouth.

"A train came off the rails here last year," says the magistrate. "Now we know why . . . "

"Beg pardon?"

"I said, now we know why the train came off the rails last year . . . I understand now!"

"'That's what you're educated for, to understand, to be our protectors . . . The Lord knew what he was doing, when he gave you understanding . . . You've worked out for us the whys and wherefores, but that watchman, he's just another peasant, he has no understanding, he just grabs you by the collar and hauls you off . . . First work things out, then you can haul us off! It's as they say, if a man's a peasant, he thinks like a peasant . . . You can put down as well, your honour, that he hit me twice on the jaw and in the chest."

"When your hut was searched, they found a second nut . . . Where did you unscrew that one, and when?"

"You mean the nut that was lying under the little red chest?"

"I don't know where it was lying, but they found it in your hut. When did you unscrew that one?"

"I didn't; Ignashka, One-Eye Semyon's son, gave it me. The one under the little red chest, that is. The one in the sledge out in the yard me and Mitrofan unscrewed."

"Which Mitrofan is that?"

"Mitrofan Petrov . . . Ain't you heard of him? He makes fishing nets round here and sells them to the gents. He needs a lot of these here nuts. Reckon there must be ten to every net . . . "

"Now listen . . . Article 1081 of the Penal Code says that any damage wilfully caused to the railway, when such damage might endanger the traffic proceeding on it and the accused knew that such damage would bring about an accident—do you understand, *knew*, and you couldn't help but know what unscrewing these nuts would lead to—then the sentence is exile with hard labour."

"Well, you know best, of course . . . We're benighted folks . . . you don't expect us to understand, do you?"

"You understand perfectly! You're lying, you're putting all this on!"

"Why should I lie? You can ask in the village, if you don't believe me . . . Without a sinker you'll only catch bleak, and they're worse 'n gudgeon—you'll not catch gudgeon without a sinker, either."

"Now you're going to tell me about those spockerels again!" smiles the magistrate.

"Spockerel don't live in our parts . . . If you float your line on the water with a butterfly on it, you might catch a chub, but seldom even then."

"All right, now be quiet . . . "

There is silence. Denis shifts from foot to foot, stares at the green baize table-top, and blinks strenuously, as if he's looking into the sun rather than at a piece of cloth. The magistrate is writing quickly.

"Can I go?" asks Denis after a while.

"No. I have to take you into custody and commit you to gaol."

Denis stops blinking and, raising his thick brows, looks at the official in disbelief.

"How do you mean, gaol? I ain't got time, your honour, I've got to go the fair, I've got to pick up three roubles off Yegor for some lard—"

"Quiet, you're disturbing me."

"Gaol . . . If there was due cause I'd go, but . . . I been leading a good life . . . What do I have to go for, eh? I haven't stole anything, I haven't been fighting . . . And if it's the arrears you're worried about, your honour, then don't you believe that elder of ours . . . You ask the zemstvo gentleman what deals with us . . . He's no Christian, that elder of ours—"

"Be quiet!"

"I am being quiet . . . " mutters Denis. "And I'll swear on oath that elder fiddled our assessment . . . There are three of us brothers: Kuzma Grigoryev, Yegor Grigoryev, and me, Denis Grigoryev . . . "

"You're distracting me . . . Hey, Semyon!" shouts the magistrate. "Take him away!"

"There are three of us brothers," Denis mutters, as two brawny soldiers grab hold of him and lead him from the courtroom. "One brother doesn't have to answer for another . . . Kuzma won't pay, so you, Denis, have to answer for him . . . Call that justice! The general our old master's dead, God rest his soul, or he'd show you, you 'judges' . . . A judge must know what he's doing, not hand it out any old how . . . He can hand out a flogging if he knows he's got to, if a man's really done wrong . . . "

❖

24

Questions

1 . . . *stop pretending you're an idiot and talk some sense.*
Why have the peasant's answers (pages 21–22) annoyed the magistrate? In your answer, consider both what he says and the way he says it.
2 Denis says he does not consider himself to be a thief, but the magistrate clearly disagrees. What reasons do they have for these differing opinions?
3 Why is Denis annoyed by the watchman's behaviour?
4 Does Denis respect authority and the law?
5 Has Denis *really done wrong* (page 24)? Does he deserve the punishment given to him?

Writing

1 Tell the full story of the confrontation between Denis and the watchman. Develop your story through dialogue rather than description. Keep in mind what Denis said about the watchman (which is not necessarily true).
2 Write a story in which there is a disagreement between someone in authority and someone who has been accused of a petty crime.

Notes

page 21 *ticking:* a heavy-duty cloth originally used for making mattress covers.
beetling: the word comes from the tufted antennae of some beetles, and means projected, shaggy, scowling.
verst: a unit of measure slightly more than a kilometre; so *verst 141* is presumably a post that indicates the distance from a major city.
page 22 *perch, pike, burbot, spockerel* (and on page 24, *bleak, chub* and *gudgeon*): all species of fresh water fish.
fivestones: a game similar to "knuckles" or "jacks".
page 23 *exile with hard labour:* in the Russian system, you could be exiled to a particular area (for example, out of the city) where you were nevertheless allowed to carry on with your normal life. Exile with hard labour is more severe.
page 24 *zemstvo:* a local council; so a *zemstvo gentleman* is, presumably, an official from the council. In this case, he seems to be in charge of setting and collecting rents.

Colette
The Advice

Born in Burgundy, and educated there, Sidonie-Gabrielle Colette
(1873-1954) went to Paris after her marriage. Her works are intensely
personal, with witty and detailed observation of setting and manners.
Her early works, the "Claudine" novels, were written under her
husband's name and created a sensation by their frankness. More highly
regarded, however, are *Sido*, a tribute to her mother, and the "Chérie"
novels.

OLD Monsieur Mestre again poured one can of water on the bleeding
hearts, one on the newly planted heliotropes, and two on the
blue hydrangeas, which were always dying of thirst. He tied up the
nasturtiums, eager to climb, and with the shears he clipped the last
withered thyrsus of the lilacs with a little cry, "Ha!" and wiped the
dirt from his hands. His little garden in Auteuil, densely planted, well
watered, and neatly arranged like a too-small parlour, was overflowing
with flowers and defying the dryness of June. Up until November, it
astonished the eyes—those of the passers-by at least—for Monsieur
Mestre, stooped over his walled-in rectangle of earth for hours, tended
it from morning to night, with the doggedness of a truck farmer. He
planted, grafted, and pruned; he hunted down slugs, small suspicious-
looking spiders, the green flies, and the blight bug. When night came,
he would clap his hands together, exclaim "Ha!" and instead of dreaming
over the phlox, haunted by gray sphinx moths beneath the white wisteria
entwined with purple wisteria, and spurning the fiery geraniums, he
would turn away from his charming handiwork and go off for a smoke
in his kitchen, or stroll along the boulevards of Auteuil.

The lovely May evening had prolonged his day as amateur gardener
by an hour after dinner. The sky, the pale gravel path, the white flowers,
and the white façades held a light which did not want to end, and
mothers, standing in the doorways of the little open houses, called
in vain to their children, who preferred the dusty warm sidewalk to
their cool beds.

"Sweetheart," Monsieur Mestre called out, "I'm going out for a bit."

Their house, long owned by the modest old couple, still showed,
beneath the Virginia creeper, its faded brick. Around it, rich villas had

sprung up—Norman chalets, Louis XVI "follies," modern cubes painted China red or Egypt blue.

Old Monsieur Mestre knew every detail of the façades, every rare tree in the gardens. But his curiosity stopped there; he envied neither the towers nor the thick crystal of the bay windows, wide as the fish ponds. Covetous of his ignorance, he liked conjectures; he had named this thatched cottage, blinded by its long bignonia wig, "Guilty Love"; that turret the colour of dried blood, "Japanese Torture". A proper white construction, with yellow silk curtains, was called "the Happy Family", and Monsieur Mestre, beaming with a sense of sweet irony in front of a kind of pink-and-blue confection made of cement, marble, and exotic wood, had christened it "First Adventure".

As a "native" of the sixteenth arrondissement, he cherished the strange provincial avenues, where a trusty old tree shelters new dwellings which a storm could wash away. He walked along, stopped, patted a little girl on the head, and clicked his tongue disapprovingly at a crying child. At night, his silver hair and beard reassured the women walking home alone and they slowed their pace in order to place themselves under the protection of "this nice old gentleman."

The pink and gold sky lingered late into the starless May night. But closer to the earth, the lights in the lamps came on, and the dauntless nightingales sang overhead, above the green benches and the stone kiosks. Monsieur Mestre greeted a little two-storey house, laid out comfortably in its garden, with a friendly glance. He called it the "Brooding Hen". A light shone in a single window hung with pink curtains. At the same moment a young man, bareheaded in the fashion of the day, came out of the house, furiously slammed the door behind him, then the gate, and stood there motionless in the street, mulish, head down, eyes fixed on the lighted window in a black, dramatic stare. Monsieur Mestre smiled and gave his shoulders a little shrug.

"Another drama! And you can see right away what it's all about! We're eighteen, nineteen years old. We want to take a bite out of life with the teeth of a tiger. We want to be the master. We've had a scene with Mama and Papa, and we've run out, after some ugly words we already regret . . . And what we really want is to go back in. But our pride won't let us. Ah, youth!"

Carried along, he said in a low, fatherly voice, "Ah, youth!"

The young man spun around on his heels and looked none too kindly at the silver-haired old man, who looked at him from above, with the benevolent majesty of a fortune-teller, as he held out his arm toward the house.

" Young man, this isn't where you should be. That is."

The young man started and backed away a step.

"Oh . . . no . . . " he said dully.

"Oh, yes . . . " said Monsieur Mestre. " Will you deny the impulse you just had to go back in?"

The big dark eyes in the still-beardless face opened in disbelief. "How . . . how do you know?"

Monsieur Mestre placed a prophetic hand on the young man's shoulder. "I know quite a few things. I know . . . that you were wrong to resist the impulse that was urging you to go back in."

"Monsieur . . . " begged the pale young man, "Monsieur, I don't want, I don't ever want . . . "

" Yes, yes," scoffed the indulgent old man. "Rebellion, the flight to freedom . . . "

" Yes . . . oh, yes," sighed the adolescent. " You know everything . . . rebellion . . . escape . . . shouldn't I . . . can't I . . . "

Monsieur Mestre's hand rested on his shoulder. "Escape . . . freedom . . . It's all words! As unhappy as you are, when you get a hundred feet from here, won't you be seized again by that same force that made you stop in front of me, by the same voice crying out to you, 'Go back! I'm the truth, I'm happiness, I am where the secret to this freedom you're searching for lies, security . . . ' "

The young man interrupted Monsieur Mestre's flowery speech with a look of unspeakable hope, smiled wildly, and ran back into the house.

"Bravo," exclaimed Monsieur Mestre in a low voice, congratulating himself.

After the door slammed shut, he heard the cry of a young voice, brief, as if muffled under a kiss. He nodded his head in thanks and was walking away, happy, discreet, when the door opened again and the young man, gasping, threw himself into his arms. He had a drunken look on his face, a pallor made green by the late light of day, which seemed wonderful to Monsieur Mestre; his eyes, brimming with tears, wandered from the rose sunset to Monsieur Mestre, to the cedar tree glistening with nightingales.

" Thanks to you . . . thanks to you," he stammered.

"I don't deserve it, young man."

"If . . . if . . . " the boy interrupted, grasping him by the hands. "It's done. Thanks to you. For days and days I didn't dare. I endured everything. I cared so much for her. I knew she was lying to me, and that all those nights . . . But I didn't dare. And then by some miracle I ran into you! You set me back on the track, you made me understand that running away wouldn't do me any good, that I would be carrying my torture with me . . . You told me that deliverance, peace . . . oh, at last, peace . . . depended on doing something . . . Thank you, thank you . . . I did it. Thank you."

He let go of Monsieur Mestre's hands, started to run as though on winged, silent feet, his black hair pushed back away from his pale face. Then Monsieur Mestre felt his heart sink; he took out his handkerchief to wipe his forehead and his hands, which the feverish grip had left feeling hot and moist, and saw on his handkerchief the red marks left by his fingers.

Questions

1 What impression does Colette give of Monsieur Mestre in the first page of the story?
2 *Covetous of his ignorance, he liked conjectures. . .* (page 27). Monsieur Mestre would rather make up stories about people than know the truth about them. What could he have been imagining when he gave houses the names "Guilty Love", "Japanese Torture" and "the Happy Family"?

3 How did people in the street react to Monsieur Mestre?
4 Explain the meaning of these lines:
   (a) *We want to take a bite out of life with the teeth of a tiger.*
   (page 27)
   (b) *... with the benevolent majesty of a fortune teller ...* (page 27)
5 *"Bravo" exclaimed Monsieur Mestre ... congratulating himself.* (page 29)
   Why is he congratulating himself?
6 In the last paragraph we discover what the young man has really done. Look back over the story and explain the difference between what was going through Monsieur Mestre's mind as he spoke to the young man, and the young man's interpretation of the words.
7 Who would you blame for the murder? Refer to particular sentences in the text to support your view.

Writing

Write a story of your own in which the main character's well-intentioned interference has disastrous consequences for others. As well as words and actions, use the sights and sounds of the location of your story to help give the reader an impression of the characters.

Notes

page 26 *thyrsus:* a botanical term for a cluster of small flowers, especially of the lilac.
Auteuil: a suburb in the western part of Paris.
defying the dryness of June: the flowers are so well cared for that they are not starting to wither as spring ends and summer approaches.
truck farmer: market gardener (US). Another term on this page which suggests that this is an American translation is *sidewalk.*

page 27 *Norman chalets, Louis XVI "follies", modern cubes:* in other words, the area had a mixture of architectural styles—all somewhat pretentious.
bignonia: a genus of large spreading trees noted for their showy, trumpet-shaped flowers.
sixteenth arrondissement: a subdivision of the city of Paris (somewhat like a suburban municipality, but with fewer powers). They have no other name than the number.
mulish: like a mule; stubborn.

William Faulkner
The Liar

William Faulkner (1897-1962) was born in Oxford, Mississippi. His family was amongst the earliest settlers in the area. After service in the Canadian Flying Corps during World War I he attended university for some time, then worked at a variety of jobs for several years. His first novel was published in 1926. He worked for many years as a scriptwriter in Hollywood. His stories and novels are based largely on the rural Mississippi of his childhood and youth. He was awarded the Nobel Prize for Literature in 1949.

FOUR men sat comfortably on the porch of Gibson's store, facing the railroad tracks and two nondescript yellow buildings. The two buildings belonged to the railroad company, hence they were tidy in an impersonal way, and were painted the same prodigious yellow. The store, not belonging to the railroad company, was not painted. It squatted stolidly against a rising hill, so that the proprietor could sit at ease, spitting into the valley, and watch the smoke-heralded passing of casual trains. The store and the proprietor resembled each other, slovenly and comfortable; and it was seldom that the owner's was the only chair tilted against the wall, and his the only shavings littering the floor.

Today he had four guests. Two of these had ridden in from the hills for trivial necessities, the other two had descended from the morning's local freight; and they sat in easy amity, watching the smoke from the locomotive dwindle away down the valley.

"Who's that feller, coming up from the deepo?" spoke one at last. The others followed his gaze and the stranger mounted the path from the station under their steady provincial stare. He was roughly dressed— a battered felt hat, a coarse blue cloth jacket and corduroy trousers— a costume identical with that of at least one of the watchers.

"Never seen him before. He don't live hereabouts, that I know of," murmured the proprietor. "Any of you boys know him?"

They shook their heads. "Might be one of them hill fellers. They

stays back yonder all year round, some of 'em ain't never been out."
The speaker, a smallish man with a large round bald head and a long
saturnine face in which his two bleached eyes were innocent and keen—
like a depraved priest—continued: "Feller over to Mitchell says one
of 'em brung his whole family into town one day last month to let
'em see a train. Train blowed, and his wife and six-seven children started
milling round kind of nervous; but when she come in sight around
the bend the whole bunch broke for the woods.

"Old man Mitchell himself had drove down fer his paper, and them
hill folks run right spang over his outfit: tore his buggy all to pieces
and scart his hoss so bad it took 'em till next day noon to catch him.
Yes, sir, heard 'em whooping and hollering all night, trying to head
that hoss into something with a fence around it. They say he run right
through old Mis' Harmon's house—" The narrator broke down over
his own invention. His audience laughed too, enjoying the humour,
but tolerantly, as one laughs at a child. His fabling was well known.
And though like all peoples who live close to the soil, they were by
nature veracious, they condoned his unlimited imagination for the sake
of the humour he achieved and which they understood.

The laughter ceased, for the newcomer was near. He mounted the
shaky steps and stood among them, a dark-favoured man. "Morning,
gentlemen," he greeted them without enthusiasm.

The proprietor, as host, returned his greeting. The others muttered
something, anything, as was the custom. The stranger entered the store
and the owner rose reluctantly and luxuriously to follow him.

"Say," spoke the raconteur, "ever notice how spry Will is for trade?
See him jump up when a customer comes in, and nigh tromps his
heels off herding him inside? Minds me of the time—"

"Shet up, Ek," another told him equably. "You already told one lie
this morning. Give a man time to smoke a pipe betwixt 'em, leastways.
Mebbe that stranger'd like to hear ye. And Will'd hate to miss it, too."
The others guffawed, and spat.

Gibson and his customer returned; the proprietor sank with a sigh
into his chair and the other, bearing a piece of cheese and a paper
sack of crackers, lowered himself onto the top step, his back against
a post, partly facing them. He began his meal while they stared at
him, gravely and without offence, as children, and all whose desires
and satisfactions are simple, can.

"Say, Will," said one after a while, "you come near missing one of
Ek's yarns. Us fellers stopped him, though. Now, Ek, you kin go ahead."

"Lissen," said the one called Ek, readily, "all you boys think that ever'
time I open my mouth it's to do a little blanket stretching, but lemme
tell you something cur'ous that reely happened. 'Twas like this—"

He was interrupted. "H'y, Will, git out yer hoss medicine: Ek's took sick."

"Musta had a stroke. We kept telling him ter stay outen them sunny fields."

"Yes, sir; shows what work'll do fer you."

"No, boys, it's that licker them Simpson boys makes. Makes a man tell the truth all the time. Sho' better keep it outen the courts, or ever'body'll be in jail."

Ek had vainly striven to surmount the merriment. "You fellers don't know nothing," he roared. "Feller comes trying to tell you the truth—" They shouted him down again, and Will Gibson summed the matter up.

"Why, Ek, we ain't doubting your ability to tell the truth when it's necessary, like in court or meeting house; but they ain't no truth ever happened as entertaining as your natural talk, hey boys? He's better'n a piece in the theayter, ain't he, fellers?"

The others assented loudly, but Ek refused to be mollified. He sat in offended dignity. The others chuckled at intervals, but at last the merriment was gone and there was no sound save the stranger's methodical crunching. He, seemingly, had taken no part in the laughter. Far up the valley a train whistled; echo took the sound and toyed with it, then let it fade back into silence.

But silence was unbearable to Ek. At last it overcame his outraged dignity. "Say," he went easily into narrative, "lemme tell you something cur'ous that reely happened to me yest'day. I was over to Mitchell yest'day waiting for the early local, when I meets up with Ken Rogers, the sheriff. We passed the time of day and he says to me, what am I doing today, and I tells him I aim to ride No. 12 over home. Then he says he's looking for somebody like me, asking me wasn't I raised in the hills. I tells him I was, and how when I turned twenty-one, paw decided I had ought to wear shoes. I hadn't never worn no shoes, and was young and skittish as a colt in them days.

"Well, sir, you may believe it or not, but when they come to my pallet that morning with them new shoes, I up and lit out of there in my shirt tail and took to the woods. Paw sent word around to the neighbours and they organised a hunt same as a bear hunt, with axes and ropes and dogs. No guns, though; paw held that to shoot me would be a waste of manpower, as I could stand up to a day's work with any of 'em.

"Well, sir, it took 'em two days to git me, and they only got me then when them big man-eating hounds of Lem Haley's put me up a tree in Big Sandy bottom, twenty miles from home. And mebbe you won't believe it, but it took paw and three strong men to put them shoes on me." He led the laughter himself, which the stranger joined. "Yes, sir; them was the days. But lemmee see, I kind of got off the track. Where was I? Oh, yes. Well, the sheriff he says to me can't I go back in the hills a ways with him. And I says, well, I dunno; I got some business in Sidon to tend to today—"

"Same business you're tending to now, I reckon?" interrupted one of his audience. "Got to git back where folks believe him when he says he's telling the truth."

"Now, look-a-here," began the affronted narrator, when the proprietor interfered. "Hush up, you Lafe; let him finish his tale. G'on Ek, won't nobody bother you again."

Ek looked at him in gratitude and resumed. "Well, listen. The sheriff, he says to me, he needs a man that knows them hill folks to go in with him. Been some trouble of some kind and he wants to clear it up. But them hill people is so leary that they's liable to shoot first, before a man kin state his point. So he wants I should go along with him and kind of mollify 'em, you might say, promising to get me back in time to catch the evening train. Well; they ain't nothing I couldn't put off a day or so, so I goes with him. He's got his car all ready and a deppity waiting, so we piles in and lit out.

"It was as putty a day as I ever see and we was having a good time, laughing and talking back and forth—"

Lafe interrupted again: "Must of been, with a set of fellers't never heard your lies before."

"Be quiet, Lafe," Gibson commanded peremptorily.

"—and first thing I knew, we come to a place where the road played out altogether. 'Have to walk from here on,' sheriff says, so we runs the car off the road a ways, and struck out afoot. Well, sir, I was born and raised in them hills, but I never seen that stretch where we was before—all ridges, and gullies where you could sling a hoss off and lose him. Finally the sheriff says to me: 'Ek,' he says, 'place we're heading for is jest across that ridge. You go on over to the house, and tell Mrs Starnes who you are; and Tim and me'll go around yonder way. Probably catch Joe in his lower field. We'll meet you at the house. Might ask Mis' Starnes if she kin git us a little snack ready.'

"'All right, sheriff,' I says, 'but I don't know nobody through here.'

"'That's all right,' sheriff says, 'jest go up to the house and tell her me and Joe and Tim'll be 'long soon.' And him and Tim started on around the ridge, and I took the route he give me. Well, sir, I moseyed on up to the top of the ridge, and sho' 'nough, there was a house and a barn setting in the next valley. It didn't look like much of a farm and I just decided them Starneses was average shif'less hill folks. There was a lot of rocks on the ridge where I was, and just as I was thinking what a good place for snakes it was and starting on down to'rds the house—bzzzrrr! went something right behind me. Gentlemen, I jumped twenty foot and lit grabbing rocks. When I had throwed a couple the rattler was gone into a hole; and then I seen three others laying with their heads mashed, and I knowed I must of stumbled into a regular den of 'em. They hadn't been dead long, and from the sample I'd had I knowed how mad the others must be, so I lit a shuck out of there. But I wasn't far from the feller had killed them three, but just how close I never learnt till later.

"I dropped on down through the brush, coming to the house from behind. Down the hill from the barn and between me and the house was a spring in a rocky gully. The spring was railed off from cattle. There was gullies and rocks ever'where: I never seen such pore, rocky land—sink holes full of rocks and narrer as wells. I had to jump 'em like a goat.

"I was about half-way down the hill when I seen a feller moving down at the spring. I hadn't seen him before. He jest wasn't there when I looked once, but there he was when I looked again, rising up by the spring. He had a wooden box under his arm. I never knowed where he come from.

Knowing how skittish them hill folks are, I was jest about to sing out when he put his finger in his mouth and whistled. I thought mebbe he was calling his dog, and I was thinking to myself it was a sorry dog that never suspicioned me when I was this close, when a woman come to the back door of the house. She stood there a minute, shading her eyes and looking all around at the ridges, but she never did look to'rds the spring. Then she stepped out, toting something in her hand, and started fer the spring on the run. Then I could see she had her Sunday hat on, and that the thing in her hand was a carpetbag. Fellers, she jest flew down that hill.

"'Uh, uh,' thinks I to myself, 'they's something going on here that I don't know about, and that Starnes don't know nothing about, neither.' The sheriff seemed mighty certain he wouldn't be at home, and I never seen a man and wife go to all that trouble to go anywheres.

"Well, sir, they met at the spring. The feller had set his little box down careful, and they was clamped together like two sheep in a storm, and was a-kissing. 'Uh, uh!' thinks I, 'here's something else me and Starnes don't know nothing about, and what'd made him itch if he did.' I was higher up than them two, and I taken a look around fer sheriff and Tim, and I seen a lone feller coming down the valley. They couldn't see him a tall, but jest when I seen him, he spied them. He stopped a minute like he was studying, then he come on, not hiding exactly, but walking careful.

"Meanwhile, them two at the spring was bent over the feller's little box, and I seen her jump back and kind of squeal. Well, sir, things was getting cur'ouser and cur'ouser ever' minute, and I was a-wishing and a-griping for sheriff and Tim to git there. 'If sheriff's wanting something to clear up,' I thinks to myself, 'I got it here waiting fer him.' And about then things begun to pop.

"Them two at the spring looked up all on a sudden. They had either seen or heard the other feller; so he walked in bold as you please. The woman she kind of comes behind the first feller; then she drops her bag and makes a bee-line fer the other one, the feller that jest comes up, and tries to grab him round the neck. He flings her off and she fell flat, but jumped up and tried to grab him again.

"Well, sir, she kep' on trying to hold his arm and he kep' on a-flinging her off, all the time walking not fast but steady to'rds number one. Finally she sees she can't stop 'em, so she backed off with her hands kind of against her side, and I can see she is scared most to death. Them two fellers is about a yard apart, when number two hauled off and knocked the other one clean into the spring. He jumped up right away and grabbed up a rail from the fence that kep' cattle out of the spring. The woman hollered and grabbed at number two again, and while he was shaking her loose, number one ups and hits him over the head with his rail, and he dropped like a ox. Them hill folks has got hard heads, but it seemed to me I could hear that feller's skull bust. Leastways, he never moved again. The woman backed off, clamping her head betwixt her hands; and the feller watched him awhile, then throwed away his rail.

"Well, sir, you could of knocked me down with a straw. There I was, watching murder, skeered to move, and no sign of sheriff and Tim. I've got along fine without no law officers, but I sho' needed one then." Ek stopped, with consummate art, and gazed about on his hearers. Their eyes were enraptured on his face, the hot black gaze of the stranger seemed like a blade spitting him against the wall, like a pinned moth. The train whistled again, unheard.

"Go on, go on," breathed Gibson.

He drew his gaze from the stranger's by an effort of will, and found that the pleasant May morning was suddenly chill. For some reason he did not want to continue.

"Well, sir, I didn't know whether the feller would finish his job right then or not; seemed like he didn't know himself. And all the time the woman was like she was took by a spell. Finally he walked over and picked the unconscious feller up, and carried him about fifteen foot down the gully, then dumped him like a sack of meal into one of them narrow sink holes. And all the time the woman was watching him like she was turned to stone." The train whistled again and the locomotive came in sight, but not one turned his eyes from the narrator's face.

"Seemed like he had decided what to do now. he run back to'rds where the woman was, and I thinks, my God, he's going to kill her, too. But no, he's just after his box. He grabs it up and come back to where he had throwed the other feller. Well, sir, if I could have been cur'ous over anything right then, I would have been cur'ous over what he was a-doing now. But as it was, I was past thinking: jest goggle-eyed, like a fish when you jerk him out the water.

"And all the time this feller is fiddling with his box, standing on the edge of that sink hole. All on a sudden he helt it out from him, shaking it over the hole. Finally something all knotted and shiny like a big watch chain fell out of it and dropped, shining and twisting, into the place where the other feller was.

"Then I knowed who'd killed them rattlers."

"My God," said someone.

"Yes, sir. They'd planned to fix that there snake where number two'd stumble on it when he came in, only he come too soon for 'em."

"My God!" repeated the voice, then the one called Lafe screamed: "Look out!"

A pistol said whow, the sound slammed against the front of the store and roared across the porch. Ek rolled from his chair and thumped on the floor, tried to rise, and fell again. Lafe sprang erect, but the others sat in reft and silent amaze, watching the stranger leaping down the path towards the track and the passing train; saw him recklessly grasp a car ladder and, shaving death by inches, scramble aboard.

*   *   *

Later, when the doctor had ridden ten miles, dressed Ek's shoulder, cursed him for a fool, and gone, the four of them took him to task.

"Well, Ek, I guess you learnt your lesson. You'll know better than tell the truth again."

"Ain't it the beatingest thing? Here's a man lied his way through life fer forty years and never got a scratch, then sets out to tell the truth fer once in his life, and gets shot."

"But what was your point," Will Gibson reiterated, "in telling your fool yarn right in front of the feller that did it? Didn't you know him again?"

Ek turned his fever exasperated face to them. "I tell you that it was all a lie, ever last word of it. I wasn't nowhere near Mitchell yest'day.

They shook their heads at his obstinacy; then Gibson, seeing that they were increasing the patient's fever, drove them out. The last to go, he turned at the door for a parting shot.

"I don't know whether you were lying, or were telling the truth, but either way, you must get a whole lot of satisfaction out of this. If you were lying, you ought to be shot for telling one so prob'le that it reely happened somewhere; and if you were telling the truth, you ought to be shot for having no better sense than to blab it out in front of the man that done the killing. Either way, if you ain't learnt a lesson, I have. And that is, don't talk at all lessen you have to, and when you got to talk, tell the truth."

"Aw, get out of here," snarled Ek. And convicted of both truthfulness and stupidity, he turned his face bitterly to the wall, knowing that his veracity as a liar was gone forever.

❖

Questions

1 When is Ek telling the truth? (Consider all the stories he tells.)
2 How does Ek keep his audience interested in his stories? (Consider the type of story he tells, and the various pauses and the comments he makes in these.)
3 Look at the reference to the train whistle on page 33, and the two similar references on pages 37 and 38. What is the purpose of these?
4 What is meant by the following expressions:
   • *provincial stare* (page 31)
   • *broke down over his own invention* (page 32)
   • *his veracity as a liar* (page 39)
5 . . . *they ain't no truth ever happened as entertaining as your natural talk, hey boys? He's better'n a piece in the theayter, ain't he, fellers?* (page 33)
   What is the attraction of telling stories? In your answer, consider the attitudes of the men in this story and your own experience.

Writing

1 Write about a time when telling the truth caused trouble.
2 Write a "yarn" that you are not expecting your audience to believe, but that causes trouble because it is believed.
In both of these pieces of writing, use some of Ek's techniques for keeping your listener(s) interested.

William Faulkner

Notes

page 31 *shavings littering the floor:* the shavings would have come from whittling (carving) a piece of wood. Presumably the owner does this to pass the time while waiting for customers.
deepo: depot (railway station)

page 32 *scart his hoss:* scared his horse
tromps: tramps, stamps
guffawed and spat: spitting is used to punctuate the conversation; a sign of agreement or unity between the group.
blanket stretching: lying, stretching the truth.

page 33 *licker them Simpson boys make:* illicit liquor (presumably whisky).
the early local: a train stopping at all stations, and therefore stopping at this small station. ("No. 12" is also a train.)
pallet: a bed, usually with a straw mattress.

page 34 *leary:* suspicious
deppity: deputy sheriff
putty: pretty
moseyed: walked in a leisurely way

page 35 *lit a shuck:* went quickly
carpetbag: a bag made out of carpet-like material, similar to an overnight or sports bag.

page 37 *a-griping:* complaining

page 38 *reft:* a contraction of "bereft" (meaning, in this context, incapable of movement).
beatingest thing: the thing that beats all others; amazing

W. W. Jacobs
The Monkey's Paw

William Wymark Jacobs (1863-1943) was born in Wapping, a docklands suburb of London. He worked as a clerk in the Civil Service until the publication of his first collection of stories in 1896 led him to become a full-time writer. Many of his stories are about sailors and the sea, but he is also known for his macabre stories such as "The Monkey's Paw".

I

WITHOUT, the night was cold and wet, but in the small parlour of Laburnum Villa the blinds were drawn and the fire burned brightly. Father and son were at chess; the former, who possessed ideas about the game involving radical changes, putting his king into such sharp and unnecessary perils that it even provoked comment from the white-haired old lady knitting placidly by the fire.

"Hark at the wind," said Mr White, who, having seen a fatal mistake after it was too late, was amiably desirous of preventing his son from seeing it.

"I'm listening," said the latter, grimly surveying the board as he stretched out his hand. "Check."

"I should hardly think that he'd come tonight," said his father, with his hand poised over the board.

"Mate," replied the son.

"That's the worst of living so far out," bawled Mr White, with sudden and unlooked-for violence; "of all the beastly, slushy, out-of-the-way places to live in, this is the worst. Pathway's a bog, and the road's a torrent. I don't know what people are thinking about. I suppose because only two houses in the road are let, they think it doesn't matter."

"Never mind, dear," said his wife soothingly; "perhaps you'll win the next one."

Mr White looked up sharply, just in time to intercept a knowing glance between mother and son. The words died away on his lips, and he hid a guilty grin in his thin grey beard.

"There he is," said Herbert White, as the gate banged too loudly and heavy footsteps came toward the door.

The old man rose with hospitable haste, and opening the door, was heard condoling with the new arrival. The new arrival also condoled with himself, so that Mrs White said, "Tut, tut!" and coughed gently as her husband entered the room, followed by a tall, burly man, beady of eye and rubicund of visage.

"Sergeant-Major Morris," he said, introducing him.

The sergeant-major shook hands, and taking the proffered seat by the fire, watched contentedly while his host got out whiskey and tumblers and stood a small copper kettle on the fire.

At the third glass his eyes got brighter, and he began to talk, the little family circle regarding with eager interest this visitor from distant parts, as he squared his broad shoulders in the chair and spoke of wild scenes and doughty deeds; of wars and plagues and strange peoples.

"Twenty-one years of it," said Mr White, nodding at his wife and son. "When he went away he was a slip of a youth in the warehouse. Now look at him."

"He don't look to have taken much harm," said Mrs White politely.

"I'd like to go to India myself," said the old man, "just to look round a bit, you know."

"Better where you are," said the sergeant-major, shaking his head. He put down the empty glass, and sighing softly, shook it again.

"I should like to see those old temples and fakirs and jugglers," said the old man. "What was that you started telling me the other day about a monkey's paw or something, Morris?"

"Nothing," said the soldier hastily. "Leastways, nothing worth hearing."

"Monkey's paw?" said Mrs White curiously.

"Well, it's just a bit of what you might call magic, perhaps," said the sergeant-major offhandedly.

His three listeners leaned forward eagerly. The visitor absent-mindedly put his empty glass to his lips and then set it down again. His host filled it for him.

"To look at," said the sergeant-major, fumbling in his pocket, "it's just an ordinary little paw, dried to a mummy."

He took something out of his pocket and proffered it. Mrs White drew back with a grimace, but her son, taking it, examined it curiously.

"And what is there special about it?" inquired Mr White as he took it from his son, and having examined it, placed it upon the table.

"It had a spell put on it by an old fakir," said the sergeant-major, "a very holy man. He wanted to show that fate ruled people's lives, and that those who interfered with it did so to their sorrow. He put a spell on it so that three separate men could each have three wishes from it."

42

His manner was so impressive that his hearers were conscious that their light laughter jarred somewhat.

"Well, why don't you have three, sir?" said Herbert White cleverly.

The soldier regarded him in the way that middle age is wont to regard presumptuous youth. "I have," he said quietly, and his blotchy face whitened.

"And did you really have the three wishes granted?" asked Mrs White.

"I did," said the sergeant-major, and his glass tapped against his strong teeth.

"And has anybody else wished?" persisted the old lady.

"The first man had his three wishes. Yes," was the reply; "I don't know what the first two were, but the third was for death. That's how I got the paw."

His tones were so grave that a hush fell upon the group.

"If you've had your three wishes, it's no good to you now, then, Morris," said the old man at last. "What do you keep it for?"

The soldier shook his head. "Fancy, I suppose," he said slowly. "I did have some idea of selling it, but I don't think I will. It has caused enough mischief already. Besides, people won't buy. They think it's a fairy tale, some of them; and those who do think anything of it want to try it first and pay me afterwards."

"If you could have another three wishes," said the old man, eyeing him keenly, "would you have them?"

"I don't know," said the other. "I don't know."

He took the paw, and dangling it between his forefinger and thumb, suddenly threw it upon the fire. White, with a slight cry, stooped down and snatched it off.

"Better let it burn," said the soldier solemnly.

"If you don't want it, Morris," said the other, "give it to me."

"I won't," said his friend doggedly. "I threw it on the fire. If you keep it, don't blame me for what happens. Pitch it on the fire again like a sensible man."

The other shook his head and examined his new possession closely. "How do you do it?" he inquired.

"Hold it up in your right hand and wish aloud," said the sergeant-major, "but I warn you of the consequences."

"Sounds like the *Arabian Nights*," said Mrs White, as she rose and began to set the supper. "Don't you think you might wish for four pairs of hands for me?"

Her husband drew the talisman from his pocket, and then all three burst into laughter as the sergeant-major, with a look of alarm on his face, caught him by the arm.

"If you must wish," he said gruffly, "wish for something sensible."

Mr White dropped it back in his pocket, and placing chairs, motioned his friend to the table. In the business of supper the talisman was partly forgotten, and afterward the three sat listening in an enthralled fashion to a second instalment of the soldier's adventures in India.

"If the tale about the monkey's paw is not more truthful than those he has been telling us," said Herbert, as the door closed behind their guest, just in time for him to catch the last train, "we shan't make much out of it."

"Did you give him anything for it, father?" inquired Mrs White, regarding her husband closely.

"A trifle," said he, colouring slightly. "He didn't want it, but I made him take it. And he pressed me again to throw it away."

"Likely," said Herbert, with pretended horror. "Why, we're going to be rich, and famous, and happy. Wish to be an emperor, father, to begin with, then you can't be hen-pecked.

He darted round the table, pursued by the maligned Mrs White armed with an antimacassar.

Mr White took the paw from his pocket and eyed it dubiously. "I don't know what to wish for, and that's a fact," he said slowly. "It seems to me I've got all I want."

"If you only cleared the house, you'd be quite happy, wouldn't you?" said Herbert, with his hand on his shoulder. "Well, wish for two hundred pounds, then; that'll just do it."

His father, smiling shamefacedly at his own credulity, held up the talisman, as his son, with a solemn face, somewhat marred by a wink at his mother, sat down at the piano and struck a few impressive chords.

"I wish for two hundred pounds," said the old man distinctly.

A fine crash from the piano greeted the words, interrupted by a shuddering cry from the old man. His wife and son ran toward him.

"It moved," he cried, with a glance of disgust at the object as it lay on the floor. "As I wished, it twisted in my hand like a snake."

"Well, I don't see the money," said his son, as he picked it up and placed it on the table, "and I bet I never shall."

"It must have been your fancy, father," said his wife, regarding him anxiously.

He shook his head. "Never mind, though; there's no harm done, but it gave me a shock all the same."

They sat down by the fire again while the two men finished their pipes. Outside, the wind was higher than ever, and the old man started nervously at the sound of a door banging upstairs. A silence unusual and depressing settled upon all three, which lasted until the old couple rose to retire for the night.

"I expect you'll find the cash tied up in a big bag in the middle

of your bed," said Herbert, as he bade them goodnight, "and something horrible squatting up on top of the wardrobe watching you as you pocket your ill-gotten gains."

He sat alone in the darkness, gazing at the dying fire, and seeing faces in it. The last face was so horrible and so simian that he gazed at it in amazement. It got so vivid that, with a little uneasy laugh, he felt on the table for a glass containing a little water to throw over it. His hand grasped the monkey's paw and with a little shiver he wiped his hand on his coat and went up to bed.

II

In the brightness of the wintry sun next morning as it streamed over the breakfast table he laughed at his fears. There was an air of prosaic wholesomeness about the room which it had lacked on the previous night, and the dirty, shrivelled little paw was pitched on the sideboard with a carelessness which betokened no great belief in its virtues.

"I suppose all old soldiers are the same," said Mrs White. "The idea of our listening to such nonsense? How could wishes be granted in these days? And if they could, how could two hundred hurt you, father?"

"Might drop on his head from the sky," said the frivolous Herbert.

"Morris said the things happened so naturally," said his father, "that you might if you so wished attribute it to coincidence.

"Well, don't break into the money before I come back," said Herbert as he rose from the table. "I'm afraid it'll turn you into a mean, avaricious man, and we shall have to disown you."

His mother laughed, and following him to the door, watched him down the road; and returning to the breakfast table, was very happy at the expense of her husband's credulity. All of which did not prevent her from scurrying to the door at the postman's knock, nor prevent her from referring somewhat shortly to retired sergeant-majors of bibulous habits when she found that the post brought a tailor's bill.

"Herbert will have some more of his funny remarks, I expect, when he comes home," she said, as they sat at dinner.

"I dare say," said Mr White, pouring himself out some beer; "but for all that, the thing moved in my hand; that I'll swear to."

"You thought it did," said the old lady soothingly.

"I say it did," replied the other. "There was no thought about it; I had just— What's the matter?"

His wife made no reply. She was watching the mysterious movements of a man outside, who, peering in an undecided fashion at the house, appeared to be trying to make up his mind to enter. In mental connection with the two hundred pounds, she noticed that the stranger was well dressed, and wore a silk hat of glossy newness. Three times he paused at the gate, and then walked on again. The fourth time he stood with his hand upon it, and then with sudden resolution flung it open and walked up the path. Mrs White at the same moment placed her hands behind her, and hurriedly unfastening the strings of her apron, put that useful article of apparel beneath the cushion of her chair.

She brought the stranger, who seemed ill at ease, into the room. He gazed at her furtively, and listened in a pre-occupied fashion as the old lady apologised for the appearance of the room, and her husband's coat, a garment which he usually reserved for the garden. She then waited as patiently as her sex would permit for him to broach his business, but he was at first strangely silent.

"I—was asked to call," he said at last, and stooped and picked a piece of cotton from his trousers. "I come from 'Maw and Megins.' "

The old lady started. "Is anything the matter?" she asked breathlessly. "Has anything happened to Herbert? What is it? What is it?"

Her husband interposed. "There, there, mother," he said hastily. "Sit down, and don't jump to conclusions. You've not brought bad news, I'm sure, sir"; and he eyed the other wistfully.

"I'm sorry—" began the visitor.

"Is he hurt?" demanded the mother wildly.

The visitor bowed in assent. "Badly hurt," he said quietly, "but he is not in any pain."

"Oh, thank God!" said the old woman, clasping her hands. "Thank God for that! Thank—"

She broke off suddenly as the sinister meaning of the assurance dawned upon her and she saw the awful confirmation of her fears in the other's averted face. She caught her breath, and turning to her slower-witted husband, laid her trembling old hand upon his. There was a long silence.

"He was caught in the machinery," said the visitor at length in a low voice.

"Caught in the machinery," repeated Mr White, in a dazed fashion; "yes."

He sat staring blankly out at the window, and taking his wife's hand between his own, pressed it as he had been wont to do in their old courting days nearly forty years before.

"He was the only one left to us," he said, turning gently to the visitor. "It is hard."

The other coughed, and rising, walked slowly to the window. "The firm wished me to convey their sincere sympathy with you in your great loss," he said, without looking round. "I beg that you will understand I am only their servant and merely obeying orders."

There was no reply; the old woman's face was white, her eyes staring, and her breath inaudible; on the husband's face was a look such as his friend the sergeant might have carried into his first action.

"I was to say that Maw and Meggins disclaim all responsibility," continued the other. "They admit no liability at all, but in consideration of your son's services, they wish to present you with a certain sum as compensation."

Mr White dropped his wife's hand, and rising to his feet, gazed with a look of horror at his visitor. His dry lips shaped the words, "How much?"

"Two hundred pounds," was the answer.

Unconscious of his wife's shriek, the old man smiled faintly, put out his hands like a sightless man, and dropped, a senseless heap, to the floor.

III

In the huge new cemetery, some two miles distant, the old people buried their dead, and came back to a house steeped in shadow and silence. It was all over so quickly that at first they could hardly realise it, and remained in a state of expectation as though of something else to happen—something else which was to lighten this load, too heavy for old hearts to bear.

But the days passed, and expectation gave place to resignation— the hopeless resignation of the old, sometimes miscalled apathy. Sometimes they hardly exchanged a word, for now they had nothing to talk about, and their days were long to weariness.

It was about a week after that the old man, waking suddenly in the night, stretched out his hand and found himself alone. The room was in darkness, and the sound of subdued weeping came from the window. He raised himself in bed and listened.

"Come back," he said tenderly: "You will be cold."

"It is colder for my son," said the old woman, and wept afresh.

The sound of her sobs died away on his ears. The bed was warm, and his eyes heavy with sleep. He dozed fitfully, and then slept until a sudden wild cry from his wife awoke him with a start.

"*The paw!*" she cried wildly. "The monkey's paw!"

He started up in alarm. "Where? Where is it? What's the matter?"

She came stumbling across the room toward him. "I want it," she said quietly. "You've not destroyed it?"

"It's in the parlour, on the bracket," he replied, marvelling. "Why?"

She cried and laughed together, and bending over, kissed his cheek. "I only just thought of it," she said hysterically. "Why didn't I think of it before? Why didn't *you* think of it?"

"Think of what?" he questioned.

"The other two wishes," she replied rapidly. "We've only had one."

"Was not that enough?" he demanded fiercely.

"No," she cried triumphantly; "we'll have one more. Go down and get it quickly, and wish our boy alive again."

The man sat up in bed and flung the bedclothes from his quaking limbs. "Good God, you are mad!" he cried, aghast.

"Get it," she panted; "get it quickly, and wish— Oh, my boy, my boy!"

Her husband struck a match and lit the candle. "Get back to bed," he said unsteadily. "You don't know what you are saying."

"We had the first wish granted," said the old woman feverishly; "why not the second?"

"A coincidence," stammered the old man.

"Go and get it and wish," cried his wife, quivering with excitement.

The old man turned and regarded her, and his voice shook. "He has been dead ten days, and besides he—I would not tell you else, but—I could only recognise him by his clothing. If he was too terrible for you to see then, how now?"

"Bring him back," cried the old woman, and dragged him toward the door. "Do you think I fear the child I have nursed?"

He went down in the darkness, and felt his way to the parlour, and then to the mantelpiece. The talisman was in its place, and a horrible fear that the unspoken wish might bring his mutilated son before him ere he could escape from the room seized upon him, and he caught his breath as he found that he had lost the direction of the door. His brow cold with sweat, he felt his way round the table, and groped along the wall until he found himself in the small passage with the unwholesome thing in his hand.

Even his wife's face seemed changed as he entered the room. it was white and expectant, and to his fears seemed to have an unnatural look upon it. He was afraid of her.

"*Wish!*" she cried, in a strong voice.

"It is foolish and wicked," he faltered.

"*Wish!*" repeated his wife.

He raised his hand. "I wish my son alive again."

The talisman fell to the floor, and he regarded it fearfully. Then he sank trembling into a chair as the old woman, with burning eyes, walked to the window and raised the blind.

He sat until he was chilled with the cold, glancing occasionally at the figure of the old woman peering through the window. The candle-end, which had burned below the rim of the china candlestick, was throwing pulsating shadows on the ceiling and walls, until, with a flicker larger than the rest, it expired. The old man, with an unspeakable sense of relief at the failure of the talisman, crept back to his bed, and a minute or two afterward the old woman came silently and apathetically beside him.

Neither spoke, but lay silently listening to the ticking of the clock. A stair creaked, and a squeaky mouse scurried noisily through the wall. The darkness was oppressive, and after lying for some time screwing up his courage, he took the box of matches, and striking one went downstairs for a candle.

At the foot of the stairs the match went out, and he paused to strike another; and at the same moment a knock, so quiet and stealthy as to be scarcely audible, sounded on the front door.

The matches fell from his hand and spilled in the passage. He stood motionless, his breath suspended until the knock was repeated. Then he turned and fled swiftly back to his room and closed the door behind him. A third knock sounded through the house.

"*What's that?*" cried the old woman, starting up.

"A rat," said the old man in shaking tones—"a rat. It passed me on the stairs."

His wife sat up in bed listening. A loud knock resounded through the house.

"It's Herbert!" she screamed. "It's Herbert!"

She ran to the door, but her husband was before her, and catching her by the arm, held her tightly.

"What are you going to do?" he whispered hoarsely.

"It's my boy; it's Herbert!" she cried, struggling mechanically. "I forgot it was two miles away. What are you holding me for? Let go. I must open the door."

"For God's sake don't let it in," cried the old man, trembling.

"You're afraid of your own son," she cried struggling. "Let me go. I'm coming, Herbert; I'm coming."

There was another knock, and another. The old woman with a sudden wrench broke free and ran from the room. Her husband followed to the landing, and called after her appealingly as she hurried downstairs. He heard the chain rattle back and the bottom bolt drawn slowly and stiffly from the socket. Then the old woman's voice strained and panting.

"The bolt," she cried loudly. "Come down. I can't reach it."

But her husband was on his hands and knees groping wildly on the floor in search of the paw. If he could only find it before the thing outside got in. A perfect fusillade of knocks reverberated through the house, and he heard the scraping of a chair as his wife put it down in the passage against the door. He heard the creaking of the bolt as it came slowly back, and at the same moment he found the monkey's paw, and frantically breathed his third and last wish.

The knocking ceased suddenly, although the echoes of it were still in the house. He heard the chair drawn back, and the door opened. A cold wind rushed up the staircase, and a long loud wail of disappointment and misery from his wife gave him courage to run down to her side, and then to the gate beyond. The street lamp flickering opposite shone on a quiet and deserted road.

❖

Q u e s t i o n s

1 *The words died away on his lips, and he hid a guilty grin in his thin grey beard.* (page 41)
   Why was Mr White feeling guilty?
2 What wishes did Mr White have, and did they come true?
3 In Part III, what is the attitude of Mr White to the monkey's paw? How is this different from Mrs White's attitude?
4 Write a comparison between this story and Poe's "The Tell-Tale Heart" (pages 96–100), saying which story you prefer and why.

W r i t i n g

Write a melodramatic story using old-fashioned language and settings. It could be the story of the first or the second owner of the monkey's paw.

N o t e s

page 41   *check:* tells your opponent in the game of chess that his/her king is threatened.
   mate: short for "checkmate", an announcement to your opponent that his/her king cannot move; the end of the game.
page 42   *fakirs:* Indian religious beggars, some of whom reputedly could perform miracles.

page 43 *fancy:* for no particular reason. The word is also used on page 44, where it carries its more usual meaning of "imagination".

Arabian Nights: the collection known as *The Thousand and One Nights.* It contains stories of great and exotic adventures ("Sinbad the Sailor" is one of these stories.)

page 44 *antimacassar:* a lace mat placed over the back of chairs to keep hair oil (macassar oil) off the fabric.

page 46 *cleared the house:* paid off the house.

simian: monkey-like.

Further activity

This story contains much old-fashioned language. Prepare a glossary of words and phrases that are no longer in common use.

James Joyce
Eveline

James Joyce (1882-1941) was born in Dublin of a middle class family whose fortunes declined during his childhood and youth. After medical studies he spent most of his life in Europe. His novel *Ulysses* has become one of the most influential, if controversial, books of the twentieth century.

This story is from a collection entitled *Dubliners*. The stories were written about the year 1904, but were not published until 1912 when Joyce published them himself.

SHE sat at the window watching the evening invade the avenue. Her head was leaned against the window curtains, and in her nostrils was the odour of dusty cretonne. She was tired.

Few people passed. The man out of the last house passed on his way home; she heard his footsteps clacking along the concrete pavement and afterwards crunching on the cinder path before the new red houses. One time there used to be a field there in which they used to play every evening with other people's children. Then a man from Belfast bought the field and built houses in it—not like their little brown houses, but bright brick houses with shining roofs. The children of the avenue used to play together in that field—the Devines, the Waters, the Dunns, little Keogh the cripple, she and her brothers and sisters. Ernest, however, never played: he was too grown up. Her father used often to hunt them in out of the field with his blackthorn stick; but usually little Keogh used to keep *nix* and call out when he saw her father coming. Still they seemed to have been rather happy then. Her father was not so bad then; and besides, her mother was alive. That was a long time ago; she and her brothers and sisters were all grown up; her mother was dead. Tizzie Dunn was dead, too, and the Waters had gone back to England. Everything changes. Now she was going to go away like the others, to leave her home.

Home! She looked round the room, reviewing all its familiar objects which she had dusted once a week for so many years, wondering where on earth all the dust came from. Perhaps she would never see again those familiar objects from which she had never dreamed of being divided. And yet during all those years she had never found out the name of the priest whose yellowing photograph hung on the wall above the broken harmonium beside the coloured print of the promises made to Blessed Margaret Mary Alacoque. He had been a school friend of her father. Whenever he showed the photograph to a visitor her father used to pass it with a casual word:

"He is in Melbourne now."

She had consented to go away, to leave her home. Was that wise? She tried to weigh each side of the question. In her home anyway she had shelter and food; she had those whom she had known all her life about her. Of course she had to work hard, both in the house and at business. What would they say of her in the Stores when they found out that she had run away with a fellow? Say she was a fool, perhaps; and her place would be filled up by advertisement. Miss Gavan would be glad. She had always had an edge on her, especially whenever there were people listening.

"Miss Hill, don't you see these ladies are waiting?"

"Look lively, Miss Hill, please."

She would not cry many tears at leaving the Stores.

But in her new home, in a distant unknown country, it would not be like that. Then she would be married—she, Eveline. People would treat her with respect then. She would not be treated as her mother had been. Even now, though she was over nineteen, she sometimes felt herself in danger of her father's violence. She knew it was that that had given her the palpitations. When they were growing up he had never gone for her, like he used to go for Harry and Ernest, because she was a girl; but latterly he had begun to threaten her and say what he would do to her only for her dead mother's sake. And now she had nobody to protect her. Ernest was dead and Harry, who was in the church decorating business, was nearly always down somewhere in the country. Besides, the invariable squabble for money on Saturday nights had begun to weary her unspeakably. She always gave her entire wages—seven shillings—and Harry always sent up what he could, but the trouble was to get any money from her father. He said she used to squander the money, that she had no head, that he wasn't going to give her his hard-earned money to throw about the streets, and much more, for he was usually fairly bad on Saturday night. In the end he would give her the money and ask her had she any intention of buying Sunday's dinner. Then she had to rush out as quickly as she could and do her marketing, holding her black leather purse tightly in her hand as she elbowed her way through the crowds and returning home late under her load of provisions. She had hard work to keep the house together and to see that the two young children who had been left to her charge went to school regularly and got their meals regularly. It was hard work—a hard life—but now that she was about to leave it she did not find it a wholly undesirable life.

She was about to explore another life with Frank. Frank was very kind, manly, open-hearted. She was to go away with him by the night-boat to be his wife and to live with him in Buenos Ayres, where he had a home waiting for her. How well she remembered the first time she had seen him; he was lodging in a house on the main road where she used to visit. It seemed a few weeks ago. He was standing at the gate, his peaked cap pushed back on his head and his hair tumbled forward over a face of bronze. Then they had come to know each other. He used to meet her outside the Stores every evening and see her home. He took her to see *The Bohemian Girl* and she felt elated as she sat in an unaccustomed part of the theatre with him. He was awfully fond of music and sang a little. People knew that they were courting, and, when he sang about the lass that loves a sailor, she always felt pleasantly confused. He used to call her Poppens out of fun. First of all it had been an excitement for her to have a fellow and then she had begun to like him. He had tales of distant countries. He had started as a deck boy at a pound a month on a ship of the Allan Line going out to Canada. He told her the names of the ships

he had been on and the names of the different services. He had sailed through the Straits of Magellan and he told her stories of the terrible Patagonians. He had fallen on his feet in Buenos Ayres, he said, and had come over to the old country just for a holiday. Of course, her father had found out the affair and had forbidden her to have anything to say to him.

"I know these sailor chaps," he said.

One day he had quarrelled with Frank, and after that she had to meet her lover secretly.

The evening deepened in the avenue. The white of two letters in her lap grew indistinct. One was to Harry; the other was to her father. Ernest had been her favourite, but she liked Harry too. Her father was becoming old lately, she noticed; he would miss her. Sometimes he could be very nice. Not long before, when she had been laid up for a day, he had read her out a ghost story and made toast for her at the fire. Another day, when their mother was alive, they had all gone for a picnic to the Hill of Howth. She remembered her father putting on her mother's bonnet to make the children laugh.

Her time was running out, but she continued to sit by the window, leaning her head against the window curtain, inhaling the odour of dusty cretonne. Down far in the avenue she could hear a street organ playing. She knew the air. Strange that it should come that very night to remind her of the promise to her mother, her promise to keep the home together as long as she could. She remembered the last night of her mother's illness; she was again in the close, dark room at the other side of the hall and outside she heard a melancholy air of Italy. The organ-player had been ordered to go away and given sixpence. She remembered her father strutting back into the sick-room saying:

"Damned Italians! coming over here!"

As she mused the pitiful vision of her mother's life laid its spell on the very quick of her being—that life of commonplace sacrifices closing in final craziness. She trembled as she heard again her mother's voice saying constantly with foolish insistence:

"Derevaun Seraun! Derevaun Seraun!"

She stood up in a sudden impulse of terror. Escape! She must escape! Frank would save her. He would give her life, perhaps love, too. But she wanted to live. Why should she be unhappy? She had a right to happiness. Frank would take her in his arms, fold her in his arms. He would save her.

She stood among the swaying crowd in the station at the North Wall. He held her hand and she knew that he was speaking to her, saying something about the passage over and over again. The station was full of soldiers with brown baggages. Through the wide doors of the sheds she caught a glimpse of the black mass of the boat, lying in beside the quay wall, with illumined portholes. She answered nothing. She felt her cheek pale and cold and, out of a maze of distress, she prayed to God to direct her, to show her what was her duty. The boat blew a long mournful whistle into the mist. If she went, tomorrow she would be on the sea with Frank, steaming towards Buenos Ayres. Their passage had been booked. Could she still draw back after all he had done for her? Her distress awoke a nausea in her body and she kept moving her lips in silent fervent prayer.

A bell clanged upon her heart. She felt him seize her hand:

"Come!"

All the seas of the world tumbled about her heart. He was drawing her into them: he would drown her. She gripped with both hands at the iron railing.

"Come!"

No! No! No! It was impossible. Her hands clutched the iron in frenzy. Amid the seas she sent a cry of anguish.

"Eveline! Evvy!"

He rushed beyond the barrier and called to her to follow. He was shouted at to go on, but he still called to her. She set her white face to him, passive, like a helpless animal. Her eyes gave him no sign of love or farewell or recognition.

Questions

1 (a) What are the things that are important to Eveline, and that she does not want to leave?

   (b) What are the things in your home that are important to you, and that you would find difficult to leave?

2 Why does Eveline want to go with Frank? (see pages 54–56)

3 *Her time was running out . . .* (page 56)
   In what ways is this true?

4 Why, at the end of the story, is Eveline *like a helpless animal?* (page 57)

Writing

1 Write two or three paragraphs describing a place you know. Use the opening of "Eveline" as a model. (You could conclude your paragraphs with the words "Everything changes", then write another paragraph describing the place as it is after the changes.)

2 Write a story about a person who is torn between desire and duty. Some possibilities are:

Desire	Duty
To leave school	To finish Year 12
To leave home	To look after an ill parent
To marry a person you have chosen	To marry a person approved by your parents
To pursue a new interest	To continue with your present friends' interests

Notes

page 53 *cretonne:* printed cotton cloth used mainly for furnishings.
keep nix: to keep watch; in Australia, the term was "to keep nit".

page 54 *harmonium:* a kind of reed organ, the air was usually supplied by foot treadles.
Stores: possibly a well-known department store.
seven shillings: a shilling is equivalent to ten cents.

page 55 *Buenos Ayres:* an old-fashioned spelling. The modern spelling is Buenos Aires.
The Bohemian Girl: an opera written by Irish-born Michael Balfe, whose operas were popular in the nineteenth century but are rarely (if ever) performed today.
a pound: roughly equivalent to two dollars.

page 56 *Straits of Magellan:* sea passage at the south of South America.
Patagonians: the southernmost province of Argentina was called Patagonia. Its inhabitants were thought to be completely uncivilised.
the air: the tune; the melody.
Derevaun Seraun: we have been unable to find any meaning for these (presumably Irish) words.

D.H. Lawrence
Her Turn

David Herbert Lawrence (1885-1930) was the son of a Nottinghamshire miner. He was a teacher before becoming a full time writer after his early novels were published. He spent much of his life travelling in Europe and North America. His novel *Kangaroo* (1923), written after a brief stay in Australia, is a penetrating if idiosyncratic description of Australian culture at the time. His stories, whether set in his native Nottinghamshire or the exotic settings derived from his travels, have a passionate intensity.

SHE was his second wife, and so there was between them that truce which is never held between a man and his first woman.

He was one for the women, and as such, an exception among the colliers. In spite of their prudery, the neighbour women liked him; he was big, naïve, and very courteous with them; he was so, even to his second wife.

Being a large man of considerable strength and perfect health, he earned good money in the pit. His natural courtesy saved him from enemies, while his fresh interest in life made his presence always agreeable. So he went his own way, had always plenty of friends, always a good job down pit.

He gave his wife thirty-five shillings a week. He had two grown-up sons at home, and they paid twelve shillings each. There was only one child by the second marriage, so Radford considered his wife did well.

Eighteen months ago, Bryan and Wentworth's men were out on strike for eleven weeks. During that time, Mrs Radford could neither cajole nor entreat nor nag the ten shillings strike-pay from her husband. So that when the second strike came on, she was prepared for action.

Radford was going, quite inconspicuously, to the publican's wife at the 'Golden Horn'. She is a large, easy-going lady of forty, and her husband is sixty-three, moreover crippled with rheumatism. She sits in the little bar-parlour of the wayside public-house, knitting for dear life, and sipping a very moderate glass of Scotch. When a decent man arrives at the three-foot width of bar, she rises, serves him, surveys him over, and, if she likes his looks, says:

"Won't you step inside, sir?"

If he steps inside, he will find not more than one or two men present. The room is warm, quite small. The landlady knits. She gives a few polite words to the stranger, then resumes her conversation with the man who interests her most. She is straight, highly-coloured, with indifferent brown eyes.

"What was that you asked me, Mr Radford?"

"What is the difference between a donkey's tail and a rainbow?" asked Radford, who had a consuming passion for conundrums.

"All the difference in the world," replied the landlady.

"Yes, but what special difference?"

"I s'll have to give it up again. You'll think me a donkey's head, I'm afraid."

"Not likely. But just you consider now, wheer . . . "

The conundrum was still under weigh, when a girl entered. She was swarthy, a fine animal. After she had gone out:

"Do you know who that is?" asked the landlady.

"I can't say as I do," replied Radford.

"She's Frederick Pinnock's daughter, from Stony Ford. She's courting our Willy."

"And a fine lass, too."

"Yes, fine enough, as far as that goes. What sort of a wife'll she make him, think you?"

"You just let me consider a bit," said the man. He took out a pocket-book and a pencil. The landlady continued to talk to the other guests.

Radford was a big fellow, black-haired, with a brown moustache, and darkish blue eyes. His voice, naturally deep, was pitched in his throat, and had a peculiar, tenor quality, rather husky, and disturbing. He modulated it a good deal as he spoke, as men do who talk much with women. Always, there was a certain indolence in his carriage.

"Our mester's lazy," his wife said. "There's many a bit of a jab wants doin', but get him to do it if you can."

But she knew he was merely indifferent to the little jobs, and not lazy.

He sat writing for about ten minutes, at the end of which time, he read:

"I see a fine girl full of life.

I see her just ready for wedlock,

But there's jealousy between her eyebrows

And jealousy on her mouth.

I see trouble ahead.

Willy is delicate.
She would do him no good.
She would never see when he wasn't well,
She would only see what she wanted—"
So, in phrases, he got down his thoughts. He had to fumble for expression, and therefore anything serious he wanted to say he wrote in 'poetry', as he called it.

Presently, the landlady rose, saying:
"Well, I s'll have to be looking after our mester. I s'll be in again before we close."

Radford sat quite comfortably on. In a while, he too bade the company good-night.

When he got home, at a quarter-past eleven, his sons were in bed, and his wife sat awaiting him. She was a woman of medium height, fat and sleek, a dumpling. Her black hair was parted smooth, her narrow-opened eyes were sly and satirical, she had a peculiar twang in her rather sleering voice.

"Our missis is a puss-puss," he said easily, of her. Her extraordinarily smooth, sleek face was remarkable. She was very healthy.

He never came in drunk. Having taken off his coat and his cap, he sat down to supper in his shirt-sleeves. Do as he might, she was fascinated by him. He had a strong neck, with the crisp hair growing low. Let her be angry as she would, yet she had a passion for that neck of his, particularly when she saw the great vein rib under the skin.

"I think, missis," he said, "I'd rather ha'e a smite o' cheese than this meat."

"Well, can't you get it yourself?"

"Yi, surely I can," he said, and went out to the pantry.

"I think, if yer comin' in at this time of night, you can wait on yourself," she justified herself.

She moved uneasily in her chair. There were several jam-tarts alongside the cheese on the dish he brought.

"Yi, missis, them tan-tafflins'll go down very nicely," he said.

"Oh, will they! Then you'd better help to pay for them," she said, amiably, but determined.

"Now what art after?"

"What am I after? Why, can't you think?" she said sarcastically.

"I'm not for thinkin', missis."

"No, I know you're not. But wheer's my money? You've been paid the Union today. Wheer do I come in?"

"Tha's got money, an' tha mun use it."

"Thank yer. An' 'aven't you none, as well?"

61

"I hadna, not till we was paid, not a ha'p'ny."

"Then you ought to be ashamed of yourself to say so."

"'Appen so."

"We'll go shares wi' th' Union money," she said. "That's nothing but what's right."

"We shonna. Tha's got plenty o' money as tha can use."

"Oh, all right," she said. "I will do."

She went to bed. It made her feel sharp that she could not get at him.

The next day, she was just as usual. But at eleven o'clock she took her purse and went up town. Trade was very slack. Men stood about in gangs, men were playing marbles everywhere in the streets. It was a sunny morning. Mrs Radford went into the furnisher-and-upholsterer's shop.

"There's a few things," she said to Mr Allcock, "as I'm wantin' for the house, and I might as well get them now, while the men's at home, and can shift me the furniture."

She put her fat purse on to the counter with a click. The man should know she was not wanting 'strap'. She bought linoleum for the kitchen, a new wringer, a breakfast-service, a spring mattress, and various other things, keeping a mere thirty shillings, which she tied in a corner of her handkerchief. In her purse was some loose silver.

Her husband was gardening in a desultory fashion when she got back home. The daffodils were out. The colts in the field at the end of the garden were tossing their velvety brown necks.

"Sithee here, missis," called Radford, from the shed which stood half-way down the path. Two doves in a cage were cooing.

"What have you got?" asked the woman, as she approached. He held out to her in his big, earthy hand a tortoise. The reptile was very, very slowly issuing its head again to the warmth.

"He's wakkened up betimes," said Radford.

"He's like th' men, wakened up for a holiday," said the wife. Radford scratched the little beast's scaly head.

"We pleased to see him out," he said.

They had just finished dinner, when a man knocked at the door.

"From Allcock's!" he said.

The plump woman took up the clothes-basket containing the crockery she had bought.

"Whativer hast got theer?" asked her husband.

"We've been wantin' some breakfast-cups for ages, so I went up town an' got 'em this mornin'," she replied.

He watched her taking out the crockery.

"Hm!" he said. "Tha's been on th' spend, seemly."

Again there was a thud at the door. The man had put down a roll of linoleum. Mr Radford went to look at it.

"They come rolling in!" he exclaimed.

"Who's grumbled more than you about the raggy oilcloth of this kitchen?" said the insidious, cat-like voice of the wife.

"It's all right, it's all right," said Radford.

The carter came up the entry with another roll, which he deposited with a grunt at the door.

"An' how much do you reckon this lot is?" he asked.

"Oh, they're all paid for, don't worry," replied the wife.

"Shall yer gi'e me a hand, mester?" asked the carter.

Radford followed him down the entry, in his easy, slouching way. His wife went after. His waistcoat was hanging loose over his shirt. She watched his easy movement of well being as she followed him, and she laughed to herself.

The carter took hold of one end of the wire mattress, dragged it forth.

"Well, this is a corker!" said Radford, as he received the burden.

"Now the mangle!" said the carter.

"What dost reckon tha's been up to, missis?" asked the husband.

"I said to myself last wash-day, if I had to turn that mangle again, tha'd ha'e ter wash the clothes thyself."

Radford followed the carter down the entry again. In the street, women were standing watching, and dozens of men were lounging round the cart. One officiously helped with the wringer.

"Gi've him thrippence," said Mrs Radford.

"Gi'e him thysen," replied her husband.

"I've no change under half a crown."

Radford tipped the carter, and returned indoors. He surveyed the array of crockery, linoleum, mattress, mangle and other goods crowding the house and the yard.

"Well, this is a winder!" he repeated.

"We stood in need of 'em enough," she replied.

"I hope tha's got plenty more from wheer they came from," he replied dangerously.

"That's just what I haven't." She opened her purse. "Two half-crowns, that's every copper I've got i' th' world."

He stood very still as he looked.

"It's right," she said.

There was a certain smug sense of satisfaction about her. A wave of anger came over him, blinding him. But he waited and waited. Suddenly his arm leapt up, the fist clenched, and his eyes blazed at her. She shrank away, pale and frightened. But he dropped his fist to his side, turned, and went out, muttering. He went down to the shed that stood in the middle of the garden. There he picked up the tortoise, and stood with bent head, rubbing its horny head.

She stood hesitating, watching him. Her heart was heavy, and yet there was a curious, cat-like look of satisfaction round her eyes. Then she went indoors and gazed at her new cups, admiringly.

The next week he handed over his half-sovereign without a word.

"You'll want some for yourself," she said, and she gave him a shilling. He accepted it.

❖

Questions

1 Describe Radford. In your description, consider both what Lawrence says about him and the type of conversations he has with others.

Look at the opening of the story, the events in the public house (hotel), his conversation with his wife when he returns home, and his keeping of the tortoise.
2 Describe how Mrs Radford forces her husband to hand over his strike-pay.
3 Explain what you think is going through the minds of:
(a) Mr Radford, and
(b) Mrs Radford
in the paragraph that begins: *There was a certain smug sense of satisfaction about her.* (page 64)
4 Comment on what this story suggests about Lawrence's view of the relationship between men and women. In your answer, you could begin by considering the following sentences:
* *She was his second wife, and so there was between them that truce which is never held between a man and his first woman.* (page 59)
* *There was only one child by the second marriage, so Radford considered his wife did well.* (page 59)
* *. . . Mrs Radford could neither cajole nor entreat nor nag the ten shillings strike-pay from her husband.* (page 59)
* *He modulated it [his voice] a good deal as he spoke, as men do who talk much with women.* (page 60)
* *But she knew he was merely indifferent to the little jobs, and not lazy.* (page 60)
* *"He's like th' men, wakened up for a holiday," said the wife.* (page 62)
* *"I hope tha's got plenty more from wheer they came from," he replied dangerously.* (page 64)
5 Do your sympathies for Mr or Mrs Radford change during the story? In your answer, consider the story as a whole, but the last two sentences in particular.

Writing

Write a story that shows the relationship between a man and a woman. (This need not be the same as the relationship portrayed by Lawrence.) In your story, try to include dialogue that reveals the developments in the relationship and shows the attitude of the characters towards one another and to the opposite sex in general. Avoid simple confrontation ("Yes-I-did/No-you-didn't").

Notes

page 59 *Bryan and Wentworth:* presumably the name of the company that owns the mine.

page 60 *under weigh:* means, in this context, under consideration.

page 61 *sleering:* "to sleer" means "to look askance". Presumably a sleering voice is one that is skeptical or sarcastic.
tan-tafflins: slang word meaning tarts or pastries.

page 62 *Union money:* strike pay; money collected by the Union and used to support workers who are on strike.
strap: on credit.
wringer: two rollers attached to a washing machine which squeeze the water out of the clothes. Used prior to the invention of spin dryers.

page 64 *corker:* a noun meaning something surprising; something that excludes further consideration; something that "puts the cap on" events.
mangle: two large rollers used for smoothing or pressing dry clothes such as sheets. In this story, the word seems to be used synonymously with "wringer".
half a crown: a silver coin worth two shillings and sixpence (25 cents).
winder: something unexpected.
half sovereign: a gold coin worth ten shillings (one dollar).

Further activity

Make a glossary of terms to explain the dialect used in the story.

Henry Lawson
The Drover's Wife

Henry Lawson (1867-1922) was born in the NSW goldfields town of Grenfell. His father was a Norwegian ex-sailor. His mother Louisa became an influential publisher and writer of feminist and political literature after she separated from her husband and went to live in Sydney. Henry joined her there in 1883. He soon began his career that made him perhaps the best-known Australian writer. He was a prolific and popular poet, but his poetry is not so highly regarded nowadays. His best stories were written by the first few years of the twentieth century. The latter part of his life was affected by illness associated with his alcoholism.

"The Drover's Wife" was first published in the *Bulletin* in 1892. It has had a lasting effect on the way Australians see the bush; and it has influenced writers, painters and film makers up to the present day.

THE two-roomed house is built of round timber, slabs, and stringy-bark, and floored with split slabs. A big bark kitchen standing at one end is larger than the house itself, verandah included.

Bush all round—bush with no horizon, for the country is flat. No ranges in the distance. The bush consists of stunted, rotten native apple-trees. No undergrowth. Nothing to relieve the eye save the darker green of a few she-oaks which are sighing above the narrow, almost waterless creek. Nineteen miles to the nearest sign of civilisation—a shanty on the main road.

The drover, an ex-squatter, is away with sheep. His wife and children are left here alone.

Four ragged, dried-up-looking children are playing about the house. Suddenly one of them yells: "Snake! Mother, here's a snake!"

The gaunt, sun-browned bushwoman dashes from the kitchen, snatches her baby from the ground, holds it on her left hip, and reaches for a stick.

"Where is it?"

"Here! gone into the wood-heap!" yells the eldest boy—a sharp-faced, excited urchin of eleven. "Stop there, mother! I'll have him. Stand back! I'll have the beggar!"

"Tommy, come here, or you'll be bit. Come here at once when I tell you, you little wretch!"

The youngster comes reluctantly, carrying a stick bigger than himself. Then he yells, triumphantly:

"There it goes—under the house!" and darts away with club uplifted. At the same time the big, black, yellow-eyed dog-of-all-breeds, who has shown the wildest interest in the proceedings, breaks his chain and rushes after that snake. He is a moment late, however, and his nose reaches the crack in the slabs just as the end of its tail disappears. Almost at the same moment the boy's club comes down and skins the aforesaid nose. Alligator takes small notice of this and proceeds to undermine the building; but he is subdued after a struggle and chained up. They cannot afford to lose him.

The drover's wife makes the children stand together near the dog-house while she watches for the snake. She gets two small dishes of milk and sets them down near the wall to tempt it to come out; but an hour goes by and it does not show itself.

It is near sunset, and a thunderstorm is coming. The children must be brought inside. She will not take them into the house, for she knows the snake is there, and may at any moment come up through the cracks in the rough slab floor; so she carries several armfuls of firewood into the kitchen and then takes the children there. The kitchen has no floor—or, rather, an earthen one, called a "ground floor" in this part of the bush. There is a large, roughly made table in the centre of the place. She brings the children in and makes them get on this table. They are two boys and two girls—mere babies. She gives them some supper, and then, before it gets dark, she goes into the house and snatches up some pillows and bedclothes—expecting to see or lay her hand on the snake any minute. She makes a bed on the kitchen table for the children and sits down beside it to watch all night.

She has an eye on the corner, and a green sapling club laid in readiness on the dresser by her side, together with her sewing basket and a copy of the *Young Ladies' Journal*. She has brought the dog into the room.

Tommy turns in, under protest, but says he'll lie awake all night and smash that blinded snake.

His mother asks him how many times she has told him not to swear.

He has his club with him under the bedclothes, and Jacky protests:

"Mummy! Tommy's skinnin' me alive wif his club. Make him take it out."

Tommy: "Shet up, you little——! D'yer want to be bit with the snake?" Jacky shuts up.

"If yer bit," says Tommy, after a pause, "you'll swell up, an' smell,

an' turn red an' green an' blue all over till yer bust. Won't he, mother?"
"Now then, don't frighten the child. Go to sleep," she says.
The two younger children go to sleep, and now and then Jacky
complains of being "skeezed". More room is made for him. Presently
Tommy says: "Mother! listen to them (adjective) little 'possums. I'd
like to screw their blanky necks."
And Jacky protests drowsily:
"But they don't hurt us, the little blanks!"
Mother: "There, I told you you'd teach Jacky to swear." But the remark
makes her smile. Jacky goes to sleep.
Presently Tommy asks:
"Mother! Do you think they'll ever extricate the (adjective) kangaroo?"
"Lord! How am I to know, child? Go to sleep."
"Will you wake me if the snake comes out?"
"Yes. Go to sleep."
Near midnight. The children are all asleep and she sits there still,
sewing and reading by turns. From time to time she glances round
the floor and wall-plate, and whenever she hears a noise she reaches
for the stick. The thunderstorm comes on, and the wind, rushing through
the cracks in the slab wall, threatens to blow out her candle. She places
it on a sheltered part of the dresser and fixes up a newspaper to protect
it. At every flash of lightning, the cracks between the slabs gleam like
polished silver. The thunder rolls, and the rain comes down in torrents.
Alligator lies at full length on the floor, with his eyes turned towards
the partition. She knows by this that the snake is there. There are large
cracks in that wall opening under the floor of the dwelling-house.
She is not a coward, but recent events have shaken her nerves. A
little son of her brother-in-law was lately bitten by a snake, and died.
Besides, she has not heard from her husband for six months, and is
anxious about him.
He was a drover, and started squatting here when they were married.
The drought of 18— ruined him. He had to sacrifice the remnant of
his flock and go droving again. He intends to move his family into
the nearest town when he comes back, and, in the meantime, his brother,
who keeps a shanty on the main road, comes over about once a month
with provisions. The wife has still a couple of cows, one horse, and
a few sheep. The brother-in-law kills one of the sheep occasionally,
gives her what she needs of it, and takes the rest in return for other
provisions.
She is used to being left alone. She once lived like this for eighteen
months. As a girl she built the usual castles in the air; but all her
girlish hopes and aspirations have long been dead. She finds all the
excitement and recreation she needs in the *Young Ladies' Journal*,

and, Heaven help her! takes a pleasure in the fashion-plates.

Her husband is an Australian, and so is she. He is careless, but a good enough husband. If he had the means he would take her to the city and keep her there like a princess. They are used to being apart, or at least she is: "No use fretting," she says. He may forget sometimes that he is married; but if he has a good cheque when he comes back he will give most of it to her. When he had money he took her to the city several times—hired a railway sleeping compartment, and put up at the best hotels. He also bought her a buggy, but they had to sacrifice that along with the rest.

The last two children were born in the bush—one while her husband was bringing a drunken doctor, by force, to attend to her. She was alone on this occasion, and very weak. She had been ill with a fever. She prayed to God to send her assistance. God sent Black Mary—the "whitest" gin in all the land. Or, at least, God sent "King Jimmy" first, and he sent Black Mary. He put his black face round the door-post, took in the situation at a glance, and said cheerfully: "All right, Missis— I bring my old woman, she down alonga creek."

One of her children died while she was here alone. She rode nineteen miles for assistance, carrying the dead child.

* * *

It must be near one or two o'clock. The fire is burning low. Alligator lies with his head resting on his paws, and watches the wall. He is not a very beautiful dog to look at, and the light shows numerous old wounds where the hair will not grow. He is afraid of nothing on the face of the earth or under it. He will tackle a bullock as readily as he will tackle a flea. He hates all other dogs—except kangaroo-dogs—and has a marked dislike to friends or relations of the family. They seldom call, however. He sometimes makes friends with strangers. He hates snakes and has killed many, but he will be bitten some day and die; most snake-dogs end that way.

Now and then the bushwoman lays down her work and watches, and listens, and thinks. She thinks of things in her own life, for there is little else to think about.

The rain will make the grass grow, and this reminds her how she fought a bushfire once while her husband was away. The grass was long, and very dry, and the fire threatened to burn her out. She put on an old pair of her husband's trousers and beat out the flames with a green bough, till great drops of sooty perspiration stood out on her forehead and ran in streaks down her blackened arms. The sight of his mother in trousers greatly amused Tommy, who worked like a little hero by her side, but the terrified baby howled lustily for his "mummy".

The fire would have mastered her but for four excited bushmen who arrived in the nick of time. It was a mixed-up affair all round: when she went to take up the baby he screamed and struggled convulsively, thinking it was a "black man"; and Alligator, trusting more to the child's sense than his own instinct, charged furiously, and (being old and slightly deaf) did not in his excitement at first recognise his mistress's voice, but continued to hang on to the moleskins until choked off by Tommy with a saddle-strap. The dog's sorrow for his blunder, and his anxiety to let it be known that it was all a mistake, was as evident as his ragged tail and a twelve-inch grin could make it. It was a glorious time for the boys; a day to look back to, and talk about, and laugh over for many years.

She thinks how she fought a flood during her husband's absence. She stood for hours in the drenching downpour, and dug an overflow gutter to save the dam across the creek. But she could not save it. There are things that a bushwoman cannot do. Next morning the dam was broken, and her heart was nearly broken too, for she thought how her husband would feel when he came home and saw the result of years of labour swept away. She cried then.

She also fought the pleuro-pneumonia—dosed and bled the few remaining cattle, and wept again when her two best cows died.

Again, she fought a mad bullock that besieged the house for a day. She made bullets and fired at him through cracks in the slabs with an old shot-gun. He was dead in the morning. She skinned him and got seventeen-and-six for the hide.

She also fights the crows and eagles that have designs on her chickens. Her plan of campaign is very original. The children cry "Crows, Mother!" and she rushes out and aims a broomstick at the birds as though it were a gun, and says "Bung!" The crows leave in a hurry; they are cunning, but a woman's cunning is greater.

Occasionally a bushman in the horrors, or a villainous-looking sundowner, comes and nearly scares the life out of her. She generally tells the suspicious-looking stranger that her husband and two sons are at work below the dam, or over at the yard, for he always cunningly inquires for the boss.

Only last week a gallows-faced swagman—having satisfied himself that there were no men on the place—threw his swag down on the verandah and demanded tucker. She gave him something to eat; then he expressed his intention of staying for the night. It was sundown then. She got a batten from the sofa, loosened the dog, and confronted the stranger, holding the batten in one hand and the dog's collar with the other. "Now you go!" she said. He looked at her and at the dog, said "All right, mum," in a cringing tone, and left. She was a determined-

looking woman, and Alligator's yellow eyes glared unpleasantly—
besides, the dog's chawing-up apparatus greatly resembled that of the
reptile he was named after.

She has few pleasures to think of as she sits here alone by the fire,
on guard against a snake. All days are much the same to her; but on
Sunday afternoon she dresses herself, tidies the children, smartens up
baby, and goes for a lonely walk along the bush-track, pushing an old
perambulator in front of her. She does this every Sunday. She takes
as much care to make herself and the children look smart as she would
if she were going to do the block in the city. There is nothing to
see, however, and not a soul to meet. You might walk for twenty miles
along this track without being able to fix a point in your mind, unless
you are a bushman. This is because of the everlasting, maddening
sameness of the stunted trees—that monotony which makes a man
long to break away and travel as far as trains can go, and sail as far
as ships can sail—and further.

But this bushwoman is used to the loneliness of it. As a girl-wife she hated it, but now she would feel strange away from it.

She is glad when her husband returns, but she does not gush or make a fuss about it. She gets him something good to eat, and tidies up the children.

She seems contented with her lot. She loves her children, but has no time to show it. She seems harsh to them. Her surroundings are not favourable to the development of the "womanly" or sentimental side of nature.

*　*　*

It must be near morning now; but the clock is in the dwelling-house. Her candle is nearly done; she forgot that she was out of candles. Some more wood must be got to keep the fire up, and so she shuts the dog inside and hurries round to the wood-heap. The rain has cleared off. She seizes a stick, pulls it out, and—crash! the whole pile collapses.

Yesterday she bargained with a stray blackfellow to bring her some wood, and while he was at work she went in search of a missing cow. She was absent an hour or so, and the native made good use of his time. On her return she was so astonished to see a good heap of wood by the chimney that she gave him an extra fig of tobacco, and praised him for not being lazy. He thanked her and left with head erect and chest well out. He was the last of his tribe and a King; but he had built that wood-heap hollow.

She is hurt now, and tears spring to her eyes as she sits down again by the table. She takes up a handkerchief to wipe the tears away, but pokes her eyes with her bare fingers instead. The handkerchief is full of holes, and she finds that she has put her thumb through one and her forefinger through another.

This makes her laugh, to the surprise of the dog. She has a keen, very keen, sense of the ridiculous; and some time or other she will amuse bushmen with the story.

She has been amused before like that. One day she sat down "to have a good cry", as she said—and the old cat rubbed against her dress and "cried too". Then she had to laugh.

*　*　*

It must be near daylight. The room is very close and hot because of the fire. Alligator still watches the wall from time to time. Suddenly he becomes greatly interested; he draws himself a few inches nearer the partition, and a thrill runs through his body. The hair on the back of his neck begins to bristle, and the battle-light is in his yellow eyes. She knows what this means, and lays her hand on the stick. The lower end of one of the partition slabs has a large crack on both sides. An evil pair of small, bright, bead-like eyes glisten at one of these holes. The snake—a black one—comes slowly out, about a foot, and moves its head up and down. The dog lies still, and the woman sits as one fascinated. The snake comes out a foot further. She lifts her stick, and the reptile, as though suddenly aware of danger, sticks his head in through the crack on the other side of the slab and hurries to get his tail round after him. Alligator springs, and his jaws come together with a snap. He misses, for his nose is large and the snake's body close down in the angle formed by the slabs and the floor. He snaps again as the tail comes round. He has the snake now, and tugs it out eighteen inches. Thud, thud comes the woman's club on the ground. Alligator pulls again. Thud, thud. Alligator gives another pull and he has the snake out—a black brute, five feet long. The head rises to dart about, but the dog has the enemy close to the neck. He is a big, heavy dog, but quick as a terrier. He shakes the snake as though he felt the original curse in common with mankind. The eldest boy wakes up, seizes his stick, and tries to get out of bed, but his mother forces him back with a grip of iron. Thud, thud—the snake's back is broken in several places. Thud, thud—its head is crushed, and Alligator's nose skinned again.

She lifts the mangled reptile on the point of her stick, carries it to the fire, and throws it in; then piles on the wood, and watches the snake burn. The boy and dog watch, too. She lays her hand on the dog's head, and all the fierce, angry light dies out of his yellow eyes. The younger children are quieted, and presently go to sleep. The dirty-legged boy stands for a moment in his shirt, watching the fire. Presently he looks up at her, sees the tears in her eyes, and, throwing his arms round her neck, exclaims:

"Mother, I won't never go drovin', blast me if I do!"

And she hugs him to her worn-out breast and kisses him; and they sit thus together while the sickly daylight breaks over the bush.

Questions

1 What difficulties does the wife have to cope with, and how does she go about this? Mention such things as:
- the snake
- the bushfire

* flood
* animals and birds
* strangers
* medical attention.

2 *They cannot afford to lose him.* (page 68)
Why is the dog so important to the drover's wife?

3 There are some attempts by the drover's wife to keep in touch with civilisation. What are they?

4 "*. . . I won't never go drovin', blast me if I do!*" (page 74)
Why does the boy say this to his mother?

5 Throughout the story, the main character is not given a name, but is simply referred to as "the drover's wife". Why has Lawson done this?

6 Write a couple of paragraphs reviewing the story. Say briefly what it is about, and comment on its strengths.

Writing

Write a story about a person's life. Make the location of the story crucial so that it shapes the sort of life the character lives. Some possibilities are:
* a factory worker
* a resident of an affluent suburb
* a single parent
* a refugee (not necessarily in Australia)
* a migrant.

Notes

page 67   *shanty:* a small public house (hotel), usually in a rural area and frequently unlicensed.

         ex-squatter: in this story, the word "squatter" refers to any person who occupied Crown land for grazing livestock. The word has come to refer more particularly to owners of very large tracts of land—people who were regarded by some as the Australian version of the English aristocracy.

         urchin: mischievous boy.

page 68   *blinded:* a swear word, the equivalent of "bloody". Although we could expect that the people living in this environment would use rough language, swearing in this story is mild. Lawson tends to use dashes, or writes the words *blanky* or (*adjective*) when characters swear.

page 69 *wall-plate:* skirting board.

page 70 *fashion-plates:* inserts in magazines, on higher quality paper and often in colour.

the "whitest" gin: gin (also spelt "din") is a term for an Aboriginal woman. It comes from the Dhuruk (Port Jackson) language. "Whitest" is meant to be a compliment.

page 71 *a bushman in the horrors:* that is, suffering from delirium tremens (DT's); recovering from a drinking binge.

sundowner: a traveller who arrives at a homestead at sundown, when food is being prepared, in the hope of being given a meal.

page 72 *perambulator:* now always abbreviated to "pram" (c.f. omnibus abbreviated to "bus"). To perambulate is to walk.

page 73 *close:* stuffy

page 74 *he felt the original curse in common with mankind:* a reference to the serpent's role in the fall of Adam, as described in the Bible.

Further activity

What is the modern equivalent of the *Young Ladies' Journal?* What effect do you think such magazines have on women's attitudes?

Further reading

1 Murray Bail: "The Drover's Wife" in a collection entitled *The Drover's Wife and other stories.*
This modern story makes intriguing references to both the Russell Drysdale painting called "The Drover's Wife", and to Lawson's story.

2 A heavily edited version of the story was printed in the Fifth Book (that is, the one for Year 5 students) of *The Victorian Readers*, which were virtually the only collections of literature used in schools in Victoria up until the 1960s. This version can be found on pages 148–151. Compare the two versions, looking at both what has been substituted, and what has been omitted. You will need to look closely, as some of the changes (for example, the last sentence of the second paragraph) are not immediately obvious.

Katherine Mansfield
The Doll's House

Born in New Zealand, Katherine Mansfield (1888-1923) spent nearly all of her short adult life in England and Europe. Kezia and some of the other characters in this story appear frequently in her stories, especially in those published in the collection entitled *The Doll's House and other stories*. There are strong autobiographical or reminiscent elements in these stories.

WHEN dear old Mrs Hay went back to town after staying with the Burnells she sent the children a doll's house. It was so big that the carter and Pat carried it into the courtyard, and there it stayed, propped up on two wooden boxes beside the feed-room door. No harm could come to it; it was summer. And perhaps the smell of paint would have gone off by the time it had to be taken in. For really, the smell of paint coming from that doll's house ("Sweet of old Mrs Hay, of course; most sweet and generous!")—but the smell of paint was quite enough to make anyone seriously ill, in Aunt Beryl's opinion. Even before the sacking was taken off. And when it was . . .

There stood the doll's house, a dark, oily, spinach green, picked out with bright yellow. Its two solid little chimneys, glued on to the roof, were painted red and white, and the door, gleaming with yellow varnish, was like a little slab of toffee. Four windows, real windows, were divided into panes by a broad streak of green. There was actually a tiny porch, too, painted yellow, with big lumps of congealed paint hanging along the edge.

But perfect, perfect little house! Who could possibly mind the smell. It was part of the joy, part of the newness.

"Open it quickly, someone!"

The hook at the side was stuck fast. Pat prised it open with his penknife, and the whole house front swung back, and—there you were, gazing at one and the same moment into the drawing-room and dining-room, the kitchen and two bedrooms. That is the way for a house to open! Why don't all houses open like that? How much more exciting than peering through the slit of a door into a mean little hall with a hat-stand and two umbrellas! That is—isn't it?—what you long to know about a house when you put your hand on the knocker. Perhaps it is the way God opens houses at the dead of night when He is taking a quiet turn with an angel . . .

"Oh-oh!" The Burnell children sounded as though they were in despair. It was too marvellous; it was too much for them. They had never seen anything like it in their lives. All the rooms were papered. There were pictures on the walls, painted on the paper, with gold frames complete. Red carpet covered all the floors except the kitchen; red plush chairs in the drawing-room, green in the dining-room; tables, beds with real bedclothes, a cradle, a stove, a dresser with tiny plates and one big jug. But what Kezia liked more than anything, what she liked frightfully, was the lamp. It stood in the middle of the dining-room table, an exquisite little amber lamp with a white globe. It was even filled all ready for lighting, though, of course, you couldn't light it. But there was something inside that looked like oil and moved when you shook it.

The father and mother dolls, who sprawled very stiff as though they had fainted in the drawing-room, and their two little children asleep upstairs, were really too big for the doll's house. They didn't look as though they belonged. But the lamp was perfect. It seemed to smile at Kezia, to say, "I live here." The lamp was real.

The Burnell children could hardly walk to school fast enough the next morning. They burned to tell everybody, to describe, to—well—to boast about their doll's house before the schoolbell rang.

"I'm to tell," said Isabel, "because I'm the eldest. And you can join in after. But I'm to tell first."

There was nothing to answer. Isabel was bossy, but she was always right, and Lottie and Kezia knew too well the powers that went with being eldest. They brushed through the thick buttercups at the road edge and said nothing.

"And I'm to choose who's to come and see it first. Mother said I might."

For it had been arranged that while the doll's house stood in the courtyard they might ask the girls at school, two at a time, to come and look. Not to stay to tea, of course, or to come traipsing through the house. But just to stand quietly in the courtyard while Isabel pointed out the beauties, and Lottie and Kezia looked pleased . . .

But hurry as they might, by the time they had reached the tarred palings of the boys' playground the bell had begun to jangle. They only just had time to whip off their hats and fall into line before the roll was called. Never mind. Isabel tried to make up for it by looking very important and mysterious and by whispering behind her hand to the girls near her, "Got something to tell you at playtime."

Playtime came and Isabel was surrounded. The girls of her class

79

nearly fought to put their arms round her, to walk away with her, to beam flatteringly, to be her special friend. She held quite a court under the huge pine trees at the side of the playground. Nudging, giggling together, the little girls pressed up close. And the only two who stayed outside the ring were the two who were always outside, the little Kelveys. They knew better than to come anywhere near the Burnells.

For the fact was, the school the Burnell children went to was not at all the kind of place their parents would have chosen if there had been any choice. But there was none. It was the only school for miles. And the consequence was all the children of the neighbourhood, the Judge's little girls, the doctor's daughters, the store-keeper's children, the milkman's were forced to mix together. Not to speak of there being an equal number of rude, rough little boys as well. But the line had to be drawn somewhere. It was drawn at the Kelveys. Many of the children, including the Burnells, were not allowed even to speak to them. They walked past the Kelveys with their heads in the air, and as they set the fashion in all matters of behaviour, the Kelveys were shunned by everybody. Even the teacher had a special voice for them, and a special smile for the other children when Lil Kelvey came up to her desk with a bunch of dreadfully common-looking flowers.

They were the daughters of a spry, hard-working little washerwoman, who went about from house to house by the day. This was awful enough. But where was Mr Kelvey? Nobody knew for certain. But everybody said he was in prison. So they were the daughters of a washerwoman and a gaolbird. Very nice company for other people's children! And they looked it. Why Mrs Kelvey made them so conspicuous was hard to understand. The truth was they were dressed in 'bits' given to her by the people for whom she worked. Lil, for instance, who was a stout, plain child, with big freckles, came to school in a dress made from a green art-serge tablecloth of the Burnells', with red plush sleeves from the Logans' curtains. Her hat, perched on top of her high forehead, was a grown-up woman's hat, once the property of Miss Lecky, the post-mistress. It was turned up at the back and trimmed with a large scarlet quill. What a little guy she looked! It was impossible not to laugh. And her little sister, our Else, wore a long white dress, rather like a nightgown, and a pair of little boy's boots. But whatever our Else wore she would have looked strange. She was a tiny wishbone of a child, with cropped hair and enormous solemn eyes—a little white owl. Nobody had ever seen her smile; she scarcely ever spoke. She went through life holding on to Lil, with a piece of Lil's skirt screwed up in her hand. Where Lil went, our Else followed. In the playground, on the road going to and from school, there was Lil marching in front and our Else holding on behind. Only when she wanted anything, or when she was out of breath, our Else gave Lil a tug, a twitch, and Lil stopped and turned round. The Kelveys never failed to understand each other.

Now they hovered at the edge; you couldn't stop them listening. When the little girls turned round and sneered, Lil, as usual, gave her silly, shamefaced smile, but our Else only looked.

And Isabel's voice, so very proud, went on telling. The carpet made a great sensation, but so did the beds with real bedclothes, and the stove with an oven door.

When she finished Kezia broke in. "You've forgotten the lamp, Isabel."

"Oh yes," said Isabel, "and there's a teeny little lamp, all made of yellow glass with a white globe that stands on the dining-room table. You couldn't tell it from a real one."

"The lamp's best of all," cried Kezia. She thought Isabel wasn't making half enough of the little lamp. But nobody paid any attention. Isabel was choosing the two who were to come back with them that afternoon and see it. She chose Emmie Cole and Lena Logan. But when the others knew they were all to have a chance, they couldn't be nice enough to Isabel. One by one they put their arms round Isabel's waist and walked her off. They had something to whisper to her, a secret. "Isabel's *my* friend."

Only the little Kelveys moved away forgotten; there was nothing more for them to hear.

Days passed and as more children saw the doll's house, the fame of it spread. It became the one subject, the rage. The one question was, "Have you seen Burnells' doll's house? Oh, ain't it lovely!" "Haven't you seen it? Oh, I say!"

Even the dinner hour was given up to talking about it. The little girls sat under the pines eating their thick mutton sandwiches and big slabs of johnny cake spread with butter. While always, as near as they could get, sat the Kelveys, our Else holding on to Lil, listening too, while they chewed their jam sandwiches out of a newspaper soaked with large red blobs.

"Mother," said Kezia, "can't I ask the Kelveys just once?"

"Certainly not, Kezia."

"But why not?"

"Run away, Kezia; you know quite well why not."

At last everybody had seen it except them. On that day the subject rather flagged. It was the dinner hour. The children stood together under the pine trees, and suddenly, as they looked at the Kelveys eating out of their paper, always by themselves, always listening, they wanted to be horrid to them. Emmie Cole started the whisper.

"Lil Kelvey's going to be a servant when she grows up."

"O-oh, how awful!" said Isabel Burnell, and she made eyes at Emmie.

Emmie swallowed in a very meaning way and nodded to Isabel as she'd seen her mother do on those occasions.

"It's true—it's true—it's true," she said.

Then Lena Logan's little eyes snapped. "Shall I ask her?" she whispered.

"Bet you don't," said Jessie May.

"Pooh, I'm not frightened," said Lena. Suddenly she gave a little squeal and danced in front of the other girls. "Watch! Watch me! Watch me now!" said Lena. And sliding, gliding, dragging one foot, giggling behind her hand, Lena went over to the Kelveys.

Lil looked up from her dinner. She wrapped the rest quickly away. Our Else stopped chewing. What was coming now?

"Is it true you're going to be a servant when you grow up, Lil Kelvey?" shrilled Lena.

Dead silence. But instead of answering, Lil only gave her silly, shamefaced smile. She didn't seem to mind the question at all. What a sell for Lena! The girls began to titter.

Lena couldn't stand that. She put her hands on her hips; she shot forward. "Yah, yer father's in prison!" she hissed spitefully.

This was such a marvellous thing to have said that the little girls rushed away in a body, deeply, deeply excited, wild with joy. Someone found a long rope, and they began skipping. And never did they skip so high, run in and out so fast, or do such daring things as on that morning.

In the afternoon Pat called for the Burnell children with the buggy and they drove home. There were visitors. Isabel and Lottie, who liked visitors, went upstairs to change their pinafores. But Kezia thieved out at the back. Nobody was about; she began to swing on the big white gates of the courtyard. Presently, looking along the road, she saw two little dots. They grew bigger, they were coming towards her. Now she could see that one was in front and one close behind. Now she could see that they were the Kelveys. Kezia stopped swinging. She slipped off the gate as if she was going to run away. Then she hesitated. The Kelveys came nearer, and beside them walked their shadows, very long, stretching right across the road with their heads in the buttercups. Kezia clambered back on the gate; she had made up her mind; she swung out.

"Hullo," she said to the passing Kelveys.

They were so astounded that they stopped. Lil gave her silly smile. Our Else stared.

"You can come and see our doll's house if you want to," said Kezia, and she dragged one toe on the ground. But at that Lil turned red and shook her head quickly.

"Why not?" asked Kezia.

Lil gasped, then said, "Your ma told our ma you wasn't to speak to us."

"Oh, well," said Kezia. She didn't know what to reply. "It doesn't matter. You can come and see our doll's house all the same. Come on. Nobody's looking."

But Lil shook her head still harder.

"Don't you want to?" asked Kezia.

Suddenly there was a twitch, a tug at Lil's skirt. She turned round. Our Else was looking at her with big, imploring eyes; she was frowning; she wanted to go. For a moment Lil looked at our Else very doubtfully. But then our Else twitched her skirt again. She started forward. Kezia led the way. Like two little stray cats they followed across the courtyard to where the doll's house stood.

"There it is," said Kezia.

There was a pause. Lil breathed loudly, almost snorted; our Else was still as stone.

"I'll open it for you," said Kezia kindly. She undid the hook and they looked inside.

"There's the drawing-room and the dining-room, and that's the—"

"Kezia!"

It was Aunt Beryl's voice. They turned round. At the back door stood Aunt Beryl, staring as if she couldn't believe what she saw.

"How dare you ask the little Kelveys into the courtyard!" said her cold, furious voice. "You know as well as I do, you're not allowed to talk to them. Run away, children, run away at once. And don't come back again," said Aunt Beryl. And she stepped into the yard and shooed them out as if they were chickens.

"Off you go immediately!" she called, cold and proud.

They did not need telling twice. Burning with shame, shrinking together, Lil huddling along like her mother, our Else dazed, somehow they crossed the big courtyard and squeezed through the white gate.

"Wicked, disobedient little girl!" said Aunt Beryl bitterly to Kezia and she slammed the doll's house to.

The afternoon had been awful. A letter had come from Willie Brent, a terrifying threatening letter, saying if she did not meet him that evening in Pulman's Bush, he'd come to the front door and ask the reason why! But now that she had frightened those little rats of Kelveys and given Kezia a good scolding, her heart felt lighter. That ghastly pressure was gone. She went back to the house humming.

When the Kelveys were well out of sight of Burnells', they sat down to rest on a big red drainpipe by the side of the road. Lil's cheeks were still burning; she took off the hat with the quill and held it on her knee. Dreamily they looked over the hay paddocks, past the creek, to the group of wattles where Logan's cows stood waiting to be milked. What were their thoughts?

Presently our Else nudged up close to her sister. But now she had forgotten the cross lady. She put out a finger and stroked her sister's quill; she smiled her rare smile.

"I seen the little lamp," she said softly.

Then both were silent once more.

❖

Questions

1 What details are there in the story that show the status of the Kelvey children? (Look at their background, speech, clothes, lunch, etc.)

2 *Even the teacher had a special voice for them, and a special smile for the other children when Lil Kelvey came up to her desk with a bunch of dreadfully common-looking flowers.* (page 80)
Describe the voice the teacher might have used to speak to the Kelveys, and the smile she gave to the other children. (You will need to think about the teacher's attitude to the children before you answer.)

3 (a) In what ways are the Kelvey children treated cruelly by the other children?
 (b) Is Kezia as cruel as the other children? (Refer to the text to support your answer.)

4 (a) Why are the children *wild with joy* (page 82) after Lena speaks to the Kelveys?
 (b) What similarities are there between the children's feelings and those of Beryl when her *heart felt lighter* (page 83)?

5 How do you respond to the characters in this story? Comment on:
 • the Kelvey children
 • Kezia
 • the other children.
 Specifically, do you feel: sympathy? empathy? warmth? contempt? pity? respect? pleasure? anger? (Refer to particular sentences to support your views.)

Writing

Think of an incident in your own childhood in which others (or you!) seemed to take pleasure in being cruel. When describing the events, focus also on the way the people thought, spoke and behaved. Consider whether you are:

* the detached narrator
* telling the story as you are experiencing it
* telling the story in retrospect.

This involves a decision about whether you will write in the first or the third person, and whether you will use the past or present tense.

Notes

page 80 *art-serge: art* is an abbreviation of "artificial"; *serge* is a type of cloth.

her hat, perched on top of her high forehead: when Katherine Mansfield was a child in the 1890s, all children were expected to wear hats to school.

What a little guy she looked!: the guy is a reference to the scarecrow-like figure that was put on a bonfire on Guy Fawkes Night (the 5th of November). In other words, she looked a mess.

our Else: the use of "our" is a lower class English form of address which suggests, in this context, that she is different from the other children—perhaps a little simple.

page 81 *johnny cake:* damper

Further reading

1 Katherine Mansfield: "At the Bay" in a collection entitled *The Garden Party and other stories*.
  Beryl and Kezia also appear in this story, and there are some further insights into their backgrounds and characters. The story is quite long and is divided into twelve sections.
2 Janet Frame: *To the Is-land*
  Janet Frame, in this book, could almost be a Kelvey!
3 Laurie Lee: *Cider with Rosie*
  The author tells of his years growing up in Slad, a village in Cotswold, after World War I.

Guy de Maupassant
The Necklace

Guy de Maupassant (1850-1893) was born in Normandy. His godfather was the French novelist Gustave Flaubert. His first story was published in 1880. He gave up his job as a civil servant to write, producing six novels, much poetry, three volumes of travel sketches, four plays and nearly three hundred stories over the next eleven years, until becoming mentally ill. His stories are often about the ignorance of the Norman peasants and the pretensions of the middle class.

SHE was one of those attractive pretty girls, born by a freak of fortune in a lower-middle-class family. She had no dowry, no expectations, no way of getting known, appreciated, loved and married by some wealthy gentleman of good family. And she allowed herself to be married to a junior clerk in the Ministry of Public Instruction.

She dressed plainly, having no money to spend on herself. But she was as unhappy as if she had known better days. Women have no sense of caste or breeding, their beauty, their grace, and their charm taking the place of birth and family. Their natural refinement, their instinctive delicacy and adaptability are their only passport to society, and these qualities enable daughters of the people to compete with ladies of gentle birth.

She always had a sense of frustration, feeling herself born for all the refinements and luxuries of life. She hated the bareness of her flat, the shabbiness of the walls, the worn upholstery of the chairs, and the ugliness of the curtains. All these things, which another woman of her class would not even have noticed, were pain and grief to her. The sight of the little Breton maid doing her simple house-work aroused in her passionate regrets and hopeless dreams. She imagined hushed ante-rooms hung with oriental fabrics and lit by tall bronze candelabra, with two impressive footmen in knee-breeches dozing in great armchairs, made drowsy by the heat of the radiators. She imagined vast drawing-rooms, upholstered in antique silk, splendid pieces of furniture littered with priceless curios, and dainty scented boudoirs, designed for tea-time conversation with intimate friends and much sought-after society gentlemen, whose attentions every woman envies and desires.

When she sat down to dinner at the round table covered with a three-days-old cloth opposite her husband, who took the lid off the casserole with the delighted exclamation: "Ah! hot-pot again! How lovely! It's the best dish in the world!", she was dreaming of luxurious dinners with classical figures and exotic birds in a fairy forest; she dreamt of exquisite dishes served on valuable china and whispered compliments listened to with a sphinx-like smile, while toying with the pink flesh of a trout or the wing of a hazel-hen.

She had a rich friend who had been with her at a convent school, but she did not like going to see her now, the contrast was so painful when she went home. She spent whole days in tears; misery, regrets, hopeless longings caused her such bitter distress.

One evening her husband came home with a broad smile on his face and a large envelope in his hand: "Look!" he cried. "Here's something for you, dear!"

She tore open the envelope eagerly and pulled out a printed card with the words: "The Minister of Public Instruction and Mme Georges Ramponneau request the honour of the company of M. and Mme Loisel at the Ministry on the evening of Monday, January 18th."

Instead of being delighted as her husband had hoped, she threw the invitation pettishly down on the table, murmuring: "What's the good of this to me?"

"But I thought you'd be pleased, dear! You never go out and this is an occasion, a great occasion. I had the greatest difficulty to get the invitation. Everybody wants one: it's very select and junior clerks don't often get asked. The whole official world will be there."

She looked at him crossly and declared impatiently: "What do you think I'm to wear?"

He hadn't thought of that and stuttered. "Why! the frock you wear for the theatre. I think it's charming!"

He stopped in astonished bewilderment when he saw his wife was crying. Two great tears were running slowly down from the corners of her eyes to the corners of her mouth; he stammered: "What's the matter? What's the matter?"

But with a great effort she had controlled her disappointment and replied quietly, drying her wet cheeks: "Oh! Nothing! Only not having anything to wear I can't go to the party. Pass on the invitation to some colleague whose wife is better dressed than I."

"Look here, Mathilde! How much would a suitable frock cost, something quite simple that would be useful on other occasions later on?"

She thought for a few seconds, doing a sum and also wondering how much she could ask for without inviting an immediate refusal and an outraged exclamation from the close-fisted clerk. At last with some hesitation she replied: "I don't know exactly but I think I could manage on four hundred francs."

He went slightly pale, for this was just the amount he had put by to get a gun so that he could enjoy some shooting the following summer on the Nanterre plain with some friends who went out lark-shooting on Sundays. But he said: "Right! I'll give you four hundred francs, but try and get a really nice frock."

The date of the party was approaching and Mme Loisel seemed depressed and worried, though her dress was ready. One evening her husband said to her: "What's the matter? The last three days you've not been yourself."

She replied: "It's rotten not to have a piece of jewellery, not a stone of any kind, to wear. I shall look poverty-stricken. I'd rather not go to the party."

He answered: "But you can wear some real flowers. That's very smart this year. For ten francs you could get two or three magnificent roses."

She was not impressed. "No, there's nothing more humiliating than to look poor in a crowd of wealthy women."

But her husband suddenly cried: "What a fool you are! Go to your friend, Mme Forestier, and ask her to lend you some of her jewellery. You know her well enough to do that.'

She uttered a joyful cry: "That's a good idea! I'd never thought of it!"

Next day she went to her friend's house and explained her dilemma.

Mme Forestier went to a glass-fronted wardrobe, took out a large casket, brought it over, opened it, and said to Mme Loisel:

"Take what you like, my dear!"

First she looked at bracelets, then a pearl collar, then a Venetian cross in gold and stones, a lovely piece of work. She tried the various ornaments in front of the glass, unable to make up her mind to take them off and put them back; she kept asking: "Haven't you got anything else?"

"Yes, go on looking; I don't know what you would like."

Suddenly she found a black satin case containing a magnificent diamond necklace, and she wanted it so desperately that her heart began to thump. Her hands were shaking, as she picked it up. She put it round her throat over her high blouse and stood in ecstasy before her reflection in the glass. Then she asked hesitantly, her anxiety showing in her voice: "Could you lend me that, just that, nothing else?"

"But of course!"

She threw her arms around her friend's neck and kissed her wildly, and hurried home with her treasure.

The day of the party arrived. Mme Loisel had a triumph. She was the prettiest woman in the room, elegant, graceful, smiling, in the seventh heaven of happiness. All the men looked at her, asked who she was, and wanted to be introduced. All the private secretaries wanted to dance with her. The Minister himself noticed her.

She danced with inspired abandon, intoxicated with delight, thinking of nothing in the triumph of her beauty and the glory of her success; she was wrapped in a cloud of happiness, the result of all the compliments, all the admiration, all these awakened desires, that wonderful success so dear to every woman's heart.

She left about four in the morning. Her husband had been dozing since midnight in a small, empty drawing-room with three other gentlemen, whose wives were also enjoying themselves.

He threw over her shoulders the wraps he had brought for going home, her simple everyday coat, whose plainness clashed with the smartness of her ball dress. She was conscious of this and wanted to hurry away, so as not to be noticed by the ladies who were putting on expensive fur wraps.

Loisel tried to stop her: "Wait a minute! You'll catch cold outside. I'll call a cab."

But she would not listen and ran down the stairs. When they got into the street they could not find a cab and began to hunt for one, shouting to the drivers they saw passing in the distance. In despair they went down towards the Seine, shivering. At last, on the Embankment they found one of those old broughams that ply by night and are only seen in Paris after dark, as if ashamed of their shabbiness in the daytime. It took them back to their house in the Rue des Martyrs and they went sadly up to their flat. For her this was the end; and he was remembering that he had got to be at the office at ten o'clock.

She took off the wraps she had put round her shoulders, standing in front of the glass to see herself once more in all her glory. But suddenly she uttered a cry; the diamond necklace was no longer round her neck. Her husband, already half undressed, asked: "What's the matter?"

She turned to him in a panic: "Mme Forestier's necklace has gone!"

He stood up, dumbfounded: "What? What do you mean? It's impossible!"

They searched in the folds of her dress, in the folds of her cloak, in the pockets, everywhere; they could not find it. He asked: "Are you sure you had it on when you left the ball?"

"Yes, I fingered it in the hall at the Ministry."

"But, if you had lost it in the street, we should have heard it drop. It must be in the cab."

"Yes, it probably is. Did you take the number?"

"No! And you didn't notice it, I suppose?"

"No!"

They looked at each other, utterly crushed. Finally Loisel dressed again: "I'll go back along the way we walked and see if I can find it."

He went out and she remained in her evening dress, without the strength even to go to bed, collapsed on a chair, without a fire, her mind a blank.

Her husband returned about seven, having found nothing. He went to the police station, to the papers to offer a reward, to the cab companies, in fact anywhere that gave a flicker of hope.

She waited all day in the same state of dismay at this appalling catastrophe. Loisel came back in the evening, his face pale and lined; he had discovered nothing.

"You must write to your friend," he said, "and say you have broken the clasp of the necklace and are getting it mended. That will give us time to turn round."

So she wrote at his dictation. After a week they had lost all hope and Loisel, who had aged five years, declared: "We must do something about replacing it."

Next day they took the case which had contained the necklace to the jeweller whose name was in it. He looked up his books: "I did not sell the jewel, Madame; I must only have supplied the case."

They went from jeweller to jeweller, looking for a necklace like the other, trying to remember exactly what it was like, both of them sick with worry and anxiety.

At last in the Palais-Royal they found a diamond necklace like the one lost. Its price was forty thousand francs, but they could have it for thirty-six thousand.

So they asked the jeweller to keep it for three days. They made it a condition that he should take it back for thirty-four if the first was found before the end of February.

Loisel had got eighteen thousand francs which his father had left him; he would borrow the rest.

He borrowed one thousand francs from one, five hundred from another, one hundred here, sixty there. He gave IOU's and notes of hand on ruinous terms, going to the Jews and money-lenders of every kind. He mortgaged the whole of the rest of his life, risked his signature on bills without knowing if he would ever be able to honour it; he was tormented with anxiety about the future, with the thought of the crushing poverty about to descend upon him and the prospect of physical privations and mental agony. Then he went and collected the necklace, putting down the thirty-six thousand francs on the jeweller's counter.

When Mme Loisel took the necklace back to Mme Forestier, the latter said rather coldly: "You ought to have brought it back sooner; I might have wanted it."

She did not open the case, as her friend had feared she might. If she had detected the replacement what would she have thought? What would she have said? Would she have considered her a thief?

Now Mme Loisel learnt the grim life of the very poor. However she faced the position with heroic courage. This ghastly debt must be paid and she would pay it. They got rid of the maid; they gave up the flat and took an attic under the tiles. She did all the heavy work of the house as well as the hateful kitchen jobs. She washed up, ruining her pink nails on the coarse crockery and the bottoms of the saucepans. She washed the dirty linen and shirts and the kitchen cloths and dried them on a line. She carried the rubbish down to the street every morning and brought up the water, stopping on every floor to get her breath. And dressed as a woman of the people, she went to the fruiterer, the grocer and the butcher with her basket on her arm, bargaining in spite of their rudeness and fighting for every penny of her miserable pittance.

Every month some notes of hand had to be paid off and others renewed to gain time. Her husband worked in the evening keeping a tradesman's books and often at night he did copying at twenty-five centimes a page. This life went on for ten years.

After ten years they had paid everything back, including the interest and the accumulated compound interest.

Mme Loisel now looked an old woman. She had become the strong, tough, coarse woman we find in the homes of the poor. Her hair was neglected, her skirt was askew, her hands were red and her voice loud; she even scrubbed the floors. But sometimes, when her husband was at the office, she would sit down near the window and dream of that evening long ago, the ball at which she had been such a success.

What would have happened to her if she had not lost the necklace? Who can say? Life is such a strange thing with its changes and chances. Such a little thing can make or mar it!

One Sunday, when she had gone for a stroll in the Champs-Élysées as a change from the week's grind, she suddenly saw a lady taking a child for a walk. It was Mme Forestier, still young, still beautiful, still attractive.

Mme Loisel felt a wave of emotion. Should she speak to her? Yes, she would. Now that she had paid, she would tell her everything. Why not?

She went up to her: "Good morning, Jeanne!"

The other woman did not recognise her, surprised at being addressed

in this familiar fashion by a common woman; she stammered: "But
Madame . . . I don't know you . . . there must be some mistake."

"No! I'm Mathilde Loisel!"

Her friend exclaimed: "Oh! Poor Mathilde, how you've changed!"

"Yes, I've had a pretty grim time since I saw you last, with lots of
trouble—and it was all your fault!"

"My fault? What do you mean?"

"You remember that diamond necklace you lent me to go to the
party at the Ministry?"

"Yes, what about it?"

"Well! I lost it!"

"What! But you brought it back to me."

"I brought you back another exactly like it; and for ten years we've
been paying for it. You'll realise it hasn't been easy, for we had no
money of our own. Well, now it's all over and I'm jolly glad!"

Mme Forestier had stopped: "You say you bought a diamond necklace
to replace mine?"

"Yes! And you never spotted it, did you? They were as like as two
peas."

And she smiled with simple proud pleasure.

Mme Forestier, deeply moved, took both her hands: "Oh! my poor
Mathilde! But mine was only paste, not worth more than five hundred
francs at most!"

❖

Questions

1 What picture does de Maupassant give of Mme Loisel in the first
four paragraphs of the story?

2 Where do your sympathies lie—with M. Loisel (who wants to buy
a gun) or Mme Loisel (who wants a new dress)?

3 What does Mme Loisel most enjoy about the ball?

4 What are M. and Mme Loisel obliged to do after the loss of the
necklace, and what are the consequences of this?

5 What do you think Mme Forestier will do now that she knows a
real diamond necklace has been given to her?

6 Does your attitude towards Mme Loisel change during the story? (Use
quotations from the story in your answer).

7 Find particular sentences that illustrate de Maupassant's attitudes
towards the Loisels and their place in society. How do you respond
to his attitudes?

Writing

Write a story about people whose circumstances change dramatically, and the effect of this on them. Some possibilities are:

* a brilliant student who is caught cheating
* someone in an influential position in a company who is retrenched
* a doctor who becomes a refugee and cannot practise in his/her new country
* someone who wins a lot of money.

Notes

page 86   *dowry:* In France until early this century a woman could not expect to "marry well" unless her family could provide a substantial dowry—which could be money, property or some other valuable gifts—for her husband.

Breton maid: a native of the province of Brittany in Western France. It was a very poor area of France and so more likely to supply servants to the lower-middle classes.

page 87   *classical figures:* statues in the ancient Greek and Roman style.

sphinx-like smile: a mysterious or ambiguous smile. In Greek mythology, the Sphinx was a fearsome creature that asked riddles. The penalty for failing to answer correctly was death.

hazel-hen: also known as hazel-grouse; a game bird no longer common in France.

page 88   *Nanterre plain:* at the time of the story this was open country—it is now a suburb of Paris.

page 89   *broughams:* one-horse carriages, with two or four wheels for two or four people.

page 91   *Palais-Royal:* originally a royal palace, later converted to a shopping arcade with a garden in the centre. Colette, who wrote the story "The Advice" (see pages 26–29) lived in an apartment at the Palais-Royal.

Jews and money lenders of every kind: there was a time in Europe when only the Jews were legally allowed to lend money—Christians were forbidden to do so. By the time of this story, the situation had changed.

page 92 *an attic under the tiles:* typically, the attics in Paris were five or six floors above street level. The top floor would be the cheapest.

centimes: there are 100 centimes to a franc—25 centimes is a very small amount.

page 93 *paste:* a term for the glass-like material that is used to make imitation jewellery.

Edgar Allan Poe
The Tell-Tale Heart

Edgar Allan Poe (1809-1849) was born in Boston, USA. He was left parentless in 1811, and was raised by a wealthy Virginian merchant, John Allan, from whom he took his middle name. His personal life was chaotic and tragic, culminating in his death under mysterious circumstances. He could be said to have originated the detective story, and was the first to define a set of rules for the short story form. He said that:

* it must create a single impression
* it should be capable of being read at a single sitting
* not a word must be irrelevant, for every word must contribute to the predesigned total effect of the author
* even the opening sentence must initiate this predesigned effect and be developed unswervingly through the story
* when the author achieves the climax, the story should end, with no further explanation or secondary effects
* only characters that are absolutely essential to the predesigned effect should be introduced, and these only developed to the extent required by the story.

TRUE!—nervous—very, very dreadfully nervous I had been and am; but why *will* you say that I am mad? The disease had sharpened my senses—not destroyed—not dulled them. Above all was the sense of hearing acute. I heard all things in the heaven and in the earth. I heard many things in hell. How, then, am I mad? Hearken! and observe how healthily—how calmly I can tell you the whole story.

It is impossible to say how first the idea entered my brain; but once conceived, it haunted me day and night. Object there was none. Passion there was none. I loved the old man. He had never wronged me. He had never given me insult. For his gold I had no desire. I think it was his eye! yes, it was this! One of his eyes resembled that of a vulture— a pale blue eye, with a film over it. Whenever it fell upon me, my blood ran cold; and so by degrees—very gradually—I made up my mind to take the life of the old man, and thus rid myself of the eye forever.

Now this is the point. You fancy me mad. Madmen know nothing. But you should have seen *me.* You should have seen how wisely I proceeded—with what caution—with what foresight—with what dissimulation I went to work! I was never kinder to the old man than during the whole week before I killed him. And every night, about midnight, I turned the latch of his door and opened it—oh, so gently! And then, when I had made an opening sufficient for my head, I put in a dark lantern, all closed, closed, so that no light shone out, and then I thrust in my head. Oh, you would have laughed to see how cunningly I thrust it in! I moved it slowly—very, very slowly, so that I might not disturb the old man's sleep. It took me an hour to place my whole head within the opening so far that I could see him as he lay upon his bed. Ha!—would a madman have been so wise as this? And then, when my head was well in the room, I undid the lantern cautiously—oh, so cautiously—cautiously (for the hinges creaked)— I undid it just so much that a single thin ray fell upon the vulture eye. And this I did for seven long nights—every night just at midnight— but I found the eye always closed; and so it was impossible to do the work; for it was not the old man who vexed me, but his Evil Eye. And every morning, when the day broke, I went boldly into the chamber, and spoke courageously to him, calling him by name in a hearty tone, and inquiring how he had passed the night. So you see he would have been a very profound old man, indeed, to suspect that every night, just at twelve, I looked in upon him while he slept.

Upon the eighth night I was more than usually cautious in opening the door. A watch's minute hand moves more quickly than did mine. Never before that night had I *felt* the extent of my own powers— of my sagacity. I could scarcely contain my feelings of triumph. To think that there I was, opening the door, little by little, and he not even to dream of my secret deeds or thoughts. I fairly chuckled at the idea; and perhaps he heard me; for he moved on the bed suddenly, as if startled. Now you may think that I drew back—but no. His room was as black as pitch with the thick darkness (for the shutters were close fastened, through fear of robbers), and so I knew that he could not see the opening of the door, and I kept pushing it on steadily, steadily.

I had my head in, and was about to open the lantern, when my thumb slipped upon the tin fastening, and the old man sprang up in the bed, crying out—"Who's there?"

I kept quite still and said nothing. For a whole hour I did not move a muscle, and in the meantime I did not hear him lie down. He was still sitting up in the bed listening;—just as I have done, night after night, hearkening to the death watches in the wall.

Presently I heard a slight groan, and I knew it was the groan of mortal terror. It was not a groan of pain or of grief—oh, no!—it was the low stifled sound that arises from the bottom of the soul when overcharged with awe. I knew the sound well. Many a night, just at midnight, when all the world slept, it has welled up from my own bosom, deepening, with its dreadful echo, the terrors that distracted me. I say I knew it well, I knew what the old man felt, and pitied him, although I chuckled at heart. I knew that he had been lying awake ever since the first slight noise, when he had turned in the bed. His fears had been ever since growing upon him. He had been trying to fancy them causeless, but could not. He had been saying to himself— "It is nothing but the wind in the chimney—it is only a mouse crossing the floor," or "it is merely a cricket which has made a single chirp." Yes, he has been trying to comfort himself with these suppositions; but he had found all in vain. *All in vain*; because Death, in approaching him, had stalked with his black shadow before him, and enveloped the victim. And it was the mournful influence of the unperceived shadow that caused him to feel—although he neither saw nor heard— to *feel* the presence of my head within the room.

When I had waited a long time, very patiently, without hearing him lie down, I resolved to open a little—a very, very little crevice in the lantern. So I opened it—you cannot imagine how stealthily, stealthily— until, at length, a single dim ray, like the thread of a spider, shot from out the crevice and full upon the vulture eye.

It was open—wide, wide open—and I grew furious as I gazed upon it. I saw it with perfect distinctness—all a dull blue, with a hideous veil over it that chilled the very marrow in my bones; but I could see nothing else of the old man's face or person: for I had directed the ray as if by instinct, precisely upon the damned spot.

And now have I not told you that what you mistake for madness is but over-acuteness of the senses?—now, I say, there came to my ears a low, dull, quick sound, such as a watch makes when enveloped in cotton. I knew *that* sound well too. It was the beating of the old man's heart. It increased my fury, as the beating of a drum stimulates the soldier into courage.

But even yet I refrained and kept still. I scarcely breathed. I held the lantern motionless. I tried how steadily I could maintain the ray upon the eye. Meantime the hellish tattoo of the heart increased. It grew quicker and quicker, and louder and louder every instant. The old man's terror *must* have been extreme! It grew louder, I say, louder every moment!—do you mark me well? I have told you that I am nervous:

so I am. And now at the dead hour of the night, amid the dreadful silence of that old house, so strange a noise as this excited me to uncontrollable terror. Yet, for some minutes longer I refrained and stood still. But the beating grew louder, louder! I thought the heart must burst. And now a new anxiety seized me—the sound would be heard by a neighbour! The old man's hour had come! With a loud yell, I threw open the lantern and leaped into the room. He shrieked once—once only. In an instant I dragged him to the floor, and pulled the heavy bed over him. I then smiled gaily, to find the deed so far done. But, for many minutes, the heart beat on with a muffled sound. This, however, did not vex me; it would not be heard through the wall. At length it ceased. The old man was dead. I removed the bed and examined the corpse. Yes, he was stone, stone dead. I placed my hand upon the heart and held it there many minutes. There was no pulsation. He was stone dead. His eye would trouble me no more.

If still you think me mad, you will think so no longer when I describe the wise precautions I took for the concealment of the body. The night waned, and I worked hastily, but in silence. First of all I dismembered the corpse. I cut off the head and the arms and the legs.

I then took up three planks from the flooring of the chamber, and deposited all between the scantlings. I then replaced the boards so cleverly, so cunningly, that no human eye—not even *his*—could have detected anything wrong. There was nothing to wash out—no stain of any kind—no blood-spot whatever. I had been too wary for that. A tub had caught all—ha! ha!

When I had made an end of these labours, it was four o'clock—still dark as midnight. As the bell sounded the hour, there came a knocking at the street door. I went down to open it with a light heart,—for what had I *now* to fear? There entered three men, who introduced themselves, with perfect suavity, as officers of the police. A shriek had been heard by a neighbour during the night; suspicion of foul play had been aroused; information had been lodged at the police office, and they (the officers) had been deputed to search the premises.

I smiled,—for *what* had I to fear? I bade the gentlemen welcome. The shriek, I said, was my own in a dream. The old man, I mentioned, was absent in the country. I took my visitors all over the house. I bade them search—search *well*. I led them, at length, to *his* chamber. I showed them his treasures, secure, undisturbed. In the enthusiasm of my confidence, I brought chairs into the room, and desired them *here* to rest from their fatigues, while I myself, in the wild audacity of my perfect triumph, placed my own seat upon the very spot beneath which reposed the corpse of the victim.

The officers were satisfied. My *manner* had convinced them. I was singularly at ease. They sat, and while I answered cheerily, they chatted about familiar things. But, ere long, I felt myself getting pale and wished them gone. My head ached, and I fancied a ringing in my ears: but still they sat and still chatted. The ringing became more distinct:— it continued and became more distinct: I talked more freely to get rid of the feeling: but it continued and gained definitiveness—until, at length, I found that the noise was *not* within my ears.

No doubt I now grew *very* pale;—but I talked more fluently, and with a heightened voice. Yet the sound increased—and what could I do? It was a *low, dull, quick sound—much such a sound as a watch makes when enveloped in cotton.* I gasped for breath—and yet the officers heard it not. I talked more quickly—more vehemently; but the noise steadily increased. I arose and argued about trifles, in a high key and with violent gesticulations, but the noise steadily increased. Why *would* they not be gone? I paced the floor to and fro with heavy strides, as if excited to fury by the observation of the men—but the noise steadily increased. Oh God! what *could* I do? I foamed—I raved— I swore! I swung the chair upon which I had been sitting, and grated it upon the boards, but the noise arose over all and continually increased. It grew louder—louder—*louder!* And still the men chatted pleasantly, and smiled. Was it possible they heard not? Almighty God!—no, no! They heard!—they suspected!—they *knew!*—they were making a mockery of my horror!—this I thought, and this I think. But anything was better than this agony! Anything was more tolerable than this derision! I could bear those hypocritical smiles no longer! I felt that I must scream or die!—and now—again!—hark! louder! louder! louder! *louder!—*

"Villains!" I shrieked, "dissemble no more! I admit the deed!—tear up the planks!—here, here!—it is the beating of his hideous heart!"

❖

Questions

1 What is it in the first paragraph that suggests that the narrator is mad rather than just "dreadfully nervous"?
2 As the story progresses, the narrator tries to convince us that he is not mad, but his statements merely confirm that he is. Why?
3 (a) What is the effect of Poe's frequent use of repetition in the following paragraph:

When I had waited a long time, very patiently, without hearing him lie down, I resolved to open a little—a very, very little crevice in the lantern. So I opened it—you cannot imagine how stealthily, stealthily—until, at length, a single dim ray, like the thread of a spider, shot from out the crevice and full upon the vulture eye. (page 98)

(b) Where else is repetition used? What is its effect?
4 When do you think the police officers would have become suspicious that they were dealing with a murderer? When would they have known definitely?
5 Which part(s) of the story do you find the most horrifying?

Writing

1 Write this story as a radio or film script. Before you begin, think about the differences between the two media.
2 Write a horror story in the first person. Avoid sensationalism.

Notes

page 98 *death watches:* a type of beetle found in timber of walls.
page 99 *scantlings:* small beams of timber which support the floor boards.

Further reading

There are a number of other Poe stories in this genre, for example:
"The Fall of the House of Usher"
"The Pit and the Pendulum"
"The Cask of Amontillado"
"The Murders in the Rue Morgue"

James Thurber
The Secret Life of Walter Mitty

James Thurber (1894-1961) was born in Columbus, Ohio, USA. He grew up in a family, which, in his words, was addicted to absurdity. An accident in his childhood eventually led to his going blind. In 1927 he became associated with the magazine *New Yorker* as managing editor. He relinquished this position, preferring to be merely a contributor of stories and cartoons.

The main character in the story, Walter Mitty, is intimidated by other people, and escapes by imagining himself to be a powerful, competent hero in various situations. This story was made into a successful movie starring Danny Kaye in 1947.

"WE'RE going through!" The Commander's voice was like thin ice breaking. He wore his full-dress uniform, with the heavily braided white cap pulled down rakishly over one cold grey eye. "We can't make it, sir. It's spoiling for a hurricane, if you ask me." "I'm not asking you, Lieutenant Berg," said the Commander. "Throw on the power lights! Rev her up to 8,500! We're going through!" The pounding of the cylinders increased: ta-pocketa-pocketa-pocketa-*pocketa-pocketa*. The Commander stared at the ice forming on the pilot window. He walked over and twisted a row of complicated dials. "Switch on No. 8 auxiliary!" he shouted. "Switch on No. 8 auxiliary!" repeated Lieutenant Berg. "Full strength in No. 3 turret!" shouted the Commander. "Full strength in No. 3 turret!" The crew, bending to their various tasks in the huge, hurtling eight-engined Navy hydroplane, looked at each other and grinned. "The Old Man'll get us through," they said to one another. "The Old Man ain't afraid of Hell!" . . .

"Not so fast! You're driving too fast!" said Mrs Mitty. "What are you driving so fast for?"

"Hmm?" said Walter Mitty. He looked at his wife, in the seat beside him, with shocked astonishment. She seemed grossly unfamiliar, like a strange woman who had yelled at him in a crowd. "You were up to fifty-five," she said. "You know I don't like to go more than forty.

You were up to fifty-five." Walter Mitty drove on toward Waterbury in silence, the roaring of the SN202 through the worst storm in twenty years of Navy flying fading in the remote, intimate airways of his mind. "You're tensed up again," said Mrs Mitty. "It's one of your days. I wish you'd let Dr Renshaw look you over."

Walter Mitty stopped the car in front of the building where his wife went to have her hair done. "Remember to get those overshoes while I'm having my hair done," she said. "I don't need overshoes," said Mitty. She put her mirror back into her bag. "We've been all through that," she said, getting out of the car. "You're not a young man any longer." He raced the engine a little. "Why don't you wear your gloves? Have you lost your gloves?" Walter Mitty reached in a pocket and brought out the gloves. He put them on, but after she had turned and gone into the building and he had driven on to a red light, he took them off again. "Pick it up, brother!" snapped a cop as the light changed, and Mitty hastily pulled on his gloves and lurched ahead. He drove around the streets aimlessly for a time, and then he drove past the hospital on his way to the parking lot.

. . . "It's the millionaire banker, Wellington McMillan," said the pretty nurse. "Yes?" said Walter Mitty, removing his gloves slowly. "Who has the case?" "Dr Renshaw and Dr Benbow, but there are two specialists here, Dr Remington from New York and Mr Pritchard-Mitford from London. He flew over." A door opened down a long, cool corridor and Dr Renshaw came out. He looked distraught and haggard. "Hello, Mitty," he said. "We're having the devil's own time with McMillan, the millionaire banker and close personal friend of Roosevelt. Obstreosis of the ductal tract. Tertiary. Wish you'd take a look at him." "Glad to," said Mitty.

In the operating room there were whispered introductions: "Dr Remington, Dr Mitty. Mr Pritchard-Mitford, Dr Mitty." "I've read your book on streptothricosis," said Pritchard-Mitford, shaking hands. "A brilliant performance, sir." "Thank you," said Walter Mitty. "Didn't know you were in the States, Mitty," grumbled Remington. "Coals to Newcastle, bringing Mitford and me up here for a tertiary." "You are very kind," said Mitty. A huge, complicated machine, connected to the operating table, with many tubes and wires, began at this moment to go pocketa-pocketa-pocketa. "The new anaesthetiser is giving way!" shouted an intern. "There is no one in the East who knows how to fix it!" "Quiet, man!" said Mitty, in a low, cool voice. He sprang to the machine, which was now going pocketa-pocketa-queep-pocketa-queep. He began fingering delicately a row of glistening dials. "Give me a fountain pen!" he snapped. Someone handed him a fountain pen. He pulled a faulty piston out of the machine and inserted the pen in its place. "That will hold for ten minutes," he said. "Get on with the operation." A nurse hurried over and whispered to Renshaw, and Mitty saw the man turn pale. "Coreopsis has set in," said Renshaw nervously. "If you would take over, Mitty?" Mitty looked at him and at the craven figure of Benbow, who drank, and at the grave, uncertain faces of the two great specialists. "If you wish," he said. They slipped a white gown on him; he adjusted a mask and drew on thin gloves; nurses handed him shining . . .

"Back it up, Mac! Look out for that Buick!" Walter Mitty jammed on the brakes. "Wrong lane, Mac,' said the parking-lot attendant, looking at Mitty closely. "Gee. Yeh," muttered Mitty. He began cautiously to back out of the lane marked "Exit Only". "Leave her sit there," said the attendant. "I'll put her away." Mitty got out of the car. "Hey, better leave the key." "Oh," said Mitty, handing the man the ignition key. The attendant vaulted into the car, backed it up with insolent skill, and put it where it belonged.

They're so damn cocky, thought Walter Mitty, walking along Main Street; they think they know everything. Once he had tried to take his chains off, outside New Milford, and he had got them wound around the axles. A man had had to come out in a wrecking car and unwind them, a young, grinning garageman. Since then Mrs Mitty always made him drive to a garage to have the chains taken off. The next time, he thought, I'll wear my right arm in a sling; they won't grin at me then. I'll have my right arm in a sling and they'll see I couldn't possibly take the chains off myself. He kicked at the slush on the sidewalk. "Overshoes," he said to himself, and he began looking for a shoe store.

When he came out into the street again, with the overshoes in a box under his arm, Walter Mitty began to wonder what the other thing was his wife had told him to get. She had told him twice, before they set out from their house for Waterbury. In a way he hated these weekly trips to town—he was always getting something wrong. Kleenex, he thought, Squibb's, razor blades? No. Toothpaste, toothbrush, bicarbonate, carborundum, initiative and referendum? He gave it up. But she would remember it. "Where's the what's-its-name?" she would ask. "Don't tell me you forgot the what's-its-name." A newsboy went by shouting something about the Waterbury trial.

. . . "Perhaps this will refresh your memory." The District Attorney suddenly thrust a heavy automatic at the quiet figure on the witness stand. "Have you ever seen this before?" Walter Mitty took the gun and examined it expertly. "This is my Webley-Vickers 50.80," he said calmly. An excited buzz ran around the courtroom. The judge rapped for order. "You are a crack shot with any sort of firearms, I believe?" said the District Attorney, insinuatingly. "Objection!" shouted Mitty's attorney. "We have shown that the defendant could not have fired the

shot. We have shown that he wore his right arm in a sling on the night of the fourteenth of July." Walter Mitty raised his hand briefly and the bickering attorneys were stilled. "With any known make of gun," he said evenly, "I could have killed Gregory Fitzhurst at three hundred feet *with my left hand.*" Pandemonium broke loose in the courtroom. A woman's scream rose above the bedlam and suddenly a lovely, dark-haired girl was in Walter Mitty's arms. The District Attorney struck at her savagely. Without rising from his chair, Mitty let the man have it on the point of the chin. "You miserable cur!" . . .

"Puppy biscuit," said Walter Mitty. He stopped walking and the buildings of Waterbury rose up out of the misty courtroom and surrounded him again. A woman who was passing laughed. "He said 'Puppy biscuit'," she said to her companion. "That man said 'Puppy biscuit' to himself." Walter Mitty hurried on. He went into an A & P, not the first one he came to but a smaller one farther up the street. "I want some biscuit for small, young dogs," he said to the clerk. "Any special brand, sir?" The greatest pistol shot in the world thought a moment. "It says 'Puppies Bark for It' on the box," said Walter Mitty.

His wife would be through at the hairdresser's in fifteen minutes, Mitty saw in looking at his watch, unless they had trouble drying it; sometimes they had trouble drying it. She didn't like to get to the hotel first; she would want him to be there waiting for her as usual. He found a big leather chair in the lobby, facing a window, and he put the overshoes and the puppy biscuit on the floor beside it. He picked up an old copy of *Liberty* and sank down into the chair. "Can Germany Conquer the World Through the Air?" Walter Mitty looked at the pictures of bombing planes and of ruined streets.

. . . "The cannonading has got the wind up in young Raleigh, sir," said the sergeant. Captain Mitty looked up at him through tousled hair. "Get him to bed," he said wearily. "With the others. I'll fly alone." "But you can't, sir," said the sergeant anxiously. "It takes two men to handle that bomber and the Archies are pounding hell out of the air. Von Richtman's circus is between here and Saulier." "Somebody's got to get that ammunition dump," said Mitty. "I'm going over. Spot of brandy?" He poured a drink for the sergeant and one for himself. War thundered and whined around the dugout and battered at the door. There was a rending of wood and splinters flew through the room. "A bit of a near thing," said Captain Mitty carelessly. "The box barrage is closing in," said the sergeant. "We only live once, Sergeant," said Mitty, with his faint, fleeting smile. "Or do we?" He poured another brandy and tossed it off. "I never seen a man could hold his brandy like you, sir," said the sergeant. "Begging your pardon, sir." Captain Mitty stood up and strapped on his huge Webley-Vickers automatic. "It's forty kilometres through hell, sir," said the sergeant. Mitty finished one last brandy. "After all," he said softly, "what isn't?" The pounding of the cannon increased; there was the rat-tat-tatting of machine guns, and from somewhere came the menacing pocketa-pocketa-pocketa of the new flame-throwers. Walter Mitty walked to the door of the dugout humming "Auprès de Ma Blonde". He turned and waved to the sergeant. "Cheerio!" he said . . .

Something struck his shoulder. "I've been looking all over this hotel for you," said Mrs Mitty. "Why do you have to hide in this old chair? How did you expect me to find you?" "Things close in," said Walter Mitty vaguely. "What?" Mrs Mitty said. "Did you get the what's-its-name? The puppy biscuit? What's in that box?" "Overshoes," said Mitty. "Couldn't you have put them on in the store?" "I was thinking," said Walter Mitty. "Does it ever occur to you that I am sometimes thinking?" She looked at him. "I'm going to take your temperature when I get you home," she said.

They went out through the revolving doors that made a faintly derisive whistling sound when you pushed them. It was two blocks to the parking lot. At the drugstore on the corner she said, "Wait here for me. I forgot something. I won't be a minute." She was more than a minute. Walter Mitty lighted a cigarette. It began to rain, rain with sleet in it. He stood up against the wall of the drugstore, smoking . . . He put his shoulders back and his heels together. "To hell with the handkerchief," said Walter Mitty scornfully. He took one last drag on his cigarette and snapped it away. Then, with that faint, fleeting smile playing about his lips, he faced the firing squad; erect and motionless, proud and disdainful, Walter Mitty the Undefeated, inscrutable to the last.

❖

Questions

1 What words or events trigger Walter Mitty's flights of fancy? Discuss each one separately.
2 Why does Walter's wife seem *grossly unfamiliar* (page 102)?
3 *I was thinking . . . Does it ever occur to you that I am sometimes thinking?* (page 106)
If Mrs Mitty had known what her husband's thoughts were, would she have agreed that he was "thinking"?
4 (a) What sort of person is Mrs Mitty?
  (b) What is her relationship with her husband?
  Refer to the text to support your judgements.
5 In what sense is Walter Mitty *proud and disdainful, Walter Mitty the Undefeated, inscrutable to the last* (page 107)?

Writing

1 The situations that Walter Mitty imagines himself to be in are common situations that have been used many times in books and television shows. They are predictable in terms of both characters and events. They present an all-powerful hero who manages to overcome great difficulties. This story, however, is meant to be humorous. Take a familiar plot and exaggerate its elements the way Thurber does when he has Mitty become the pilot, the doctor, the war hero and the accused in a trial. Begin by thinking about books, films or television shows that present predictable plots.
2 Take a familiar plot, and change a significant element of it to make it funny. Imagine, for example, an 83-year-old *Rocky*, or *The Karate-Kid* with a sore hand.

James Thurber

Notes

page 102   *Old Man:* a common term to describe a commander who is respected.

page 103   *SN202:* A blend of fact and fiction. Mitty seems to be talking about a navy flying boat, but there was no such numbered plane flown by the Americans in World War I. However, the first successful sea planes were built and flown in the United States in 1911.

Roosevelt: American president from 1933 to 1945.

obstreosis of the ductal tract: Mitty is fantasising about being a brilliant surgeon, but the terms he uses are somewhat mixed. Some are real, some refer to irrelevant diseases; some are nonexistent.

Some of the more obscure references are:

obstreosis: meaningless.

streptothricosis: a tropical disease affecting hoofed animals.

coreopsis: a plant with daisy-like flowers.

coals to Newcastle: Newcastle is a coal-producing city—to take coal to it is to take something of which there is a plentiful supply; to do something which is unnecessary.

page 104   *Buick:* a make of car.

chains: placed on tyres to assist travel through ice or snow.

Waterbury: Perhaps fictitious, but there is a town of this name in Connecticut, approximately 150 kilometres north of New York City.

carborundum, initiative and referendum: Walter is trying to remember what he has to buy—three words are loosely associated in his mind because they sound alike, but their meaning is unrelated.

page 105   *A & P:* a general store

page 106   *Archies:* anti-aircraft artillery

Von Richtman's circus: this is a term made up by Mitty to describe a group of German airplanes. Perhaps it is based on the exploits of Baron Manfred von Richthofen, World War I flying ace.

box barrage: concentrated shelling of a confined area; rectangular, therefore box-shaped.

Auprès de Ma Blonde: a French soldiers' song popular in World War I. The title means "Near to my sweetheart".

Leo Tolstoy
How Much Land Does a Man Need?

Leo Tolstoy (1828-1910) was a Russian nobleman best known for his novels *War and Peace* (1866) and *Anna Karenina* (1877). He developed strong social and philosophical views in later life that led him to free the serfs on his estate and live a simple life. He became separated from his wife and family, running away from home eleven days before he died. This story was written in 1886, and was translated by Louise and Aylmer Maude.

I

AN elder sister came to visit her younger sister in the country. The elder was married to a shopkeeper in town, the younger to a peasant in the village. As the sisters sat over their tea talking, the elder began to boast of the advantages of town life, saying how comfortably they lived there, how well they dressed, what fine clothes her children wore, what good things they ate and drank, and how she went to the theatre, promenades, and entertainments.

The younger sister was piqued, and in turn disparaged the life of a shopkeeper, and stood up for that of a peasant.

"I wouldn't change my way of life for yours," said she. "We may live roughly, but at least we're free from worry. You live in better style than we do, but though you often earn more than you need, you're very likely to lose all you have. You know the proverb, 'Loss and gain are brothers twain.' It often happens that people who're wealthy one day are begging their bread the next. Our way is safer. Though a peasant's life is not a rich one, it's long. We'll never grow rich, but we'll always have enough to eat."

The elder sister said sneeringly:

"Enough? Yes, if you like to share with the pigs and the calves! What do you know of elegance or manners! However much your good man may slave, you'll die as you live—on a dung heap—and your children the same."

"Well, what of that?" replied the younger sister. "Of course our work is rough and hard. But on the other hand, it's sure, and we need not bow to anyone. But you, in your towns, are surrounded by temptations; today all may be right, but tomorrow the Evil One may tempt your husband with cards, wine, or women, and all will go to ruin. Don't such things happen often enough?"

Pahom, the master of the house, was lying on the top of the stove and he listened to the women's chatter.

"It is perfectly true," thought he. "Busy as we are from childhood tilling mother earth, we peasants have no time to let any nonsense settle in our heads. Our only trouble is that we haven't land enough. If I had plenty of land, I shouldn't fear the Devil himself!"

The women finished their tea, chatted a while about dress, and then cleared away the tea things and lay down to sleep.

But the Devil had been sitting behind the stove, and had heard all that had been said. He was pleased that the peasant's wife had led her husband into boasting, and that he had said that if he had plenty of land he would not fear the Devil himself.

"All right," thought the Devil. "We'll have a tussle. I'll give you land enough; and by means of that land I'll get you into my power."

II

Close to the village there lived a lady, a small landowner who had an estate of about three hundred acres. She had always lived on good terms with the peasants until she enaged as her manager an old soldier, who took to burdening the people with fines. However careful Pahom tried to be, it happened again and again that now a horse of his got among the lady's oats, now a cow strayed into her garden, now his calves found their way into her meadows—and he always had to pay a fine.

Pahom paid up, but grumbled, and, going home in a temper, was rough with his family. All through that summer Pahom had much trouble because of this manager, and he was actually glad when winter came and the cattle had to be stabled. Though he grudged the fodder when they could no longer graze on the pasture land, at least he was free from anxiety about them.

In the winter the news got about that the lady was going to sell her land and that the keeper of the inn on the high road was bargaining for it. When the peasants heard this they were very much alarmed.

"Well," thought they, "if the innkeeper gets the land, he'll worry us with fines worse than the lady's manager. We all depend on that estate."

So the peasants went on behalf of their village Council and asked the lady not to sell the land to the innkeeper, offering her a better price for it themselves. The lady agreed to let them have it. Then the peasants tried to arrange for the village Council to buy the whole estate, so that it might be held by them all in common. They met twice to discuss it, but could not settle the matter; the Evil One sowed discord among them and they could not agree. So they decided to buy the land individually, each according to his means; and the lady agreed to this plan as she had to the other.

Presently Pahom heard that a neighbour of his was buying fifty acres, and that the lady had consented to accept one-half in cash and to wait a year for the other half. Pahom felt envious.

"Look at that," thought he, "the land is all being sold, and I'll get none of it." So he spoke to his wife.

"Other people are buying," said he, "and we must also buy twenty acres or so. Life is becoming impossible. That manager is simply crushing us with his fines."

So they put their heads together and considered how they could manage to buy it. They had one hundred rubles laid by. They sold a colt and one half of their bees, hired out one of their sons as a farm hand, and took his wages in advance; borrowed the rest from a brother-in-law and so scraped together half the purchase money.

Having done this, Pahom chose a farm of forty acres, some of it wooded, and went to the lady to bargain for it. They came to an agreement, and he shook hands with her upon it and paid her a deposit in advance. Then they went to town and signed the deeds, he paying half the price down, and undertaking to pay the remainder within two years.

So now Pahom had land of his own. He borrowed seed, and sowed it on the land he had bought. The harvest was a good one, and within a year, he had managed to pay off his debts both to the lady and to his brother-in-law. So he became a landowner, ploughing and sowing his own land, making hay on his own land, cutting his own trees, and feeding his cattle on his own pasture. When he went out to plough his fields, or to look at his growing corn, or at his grass meadows, his heart would fill with joy. The grass that grew and the flowers that bloomed there seemed to him unlike any that grew elsewhere. Formerly, when he had passed by that land, it had appeared the same as any other land, but now it seemed quite different.

III

So Pahom was well contented, and everything would have been right if the neighbouring peasants would only not have trespassed on his wheatfields and meadows. He appealed to them most civilly, but they still went on: now the herdsmen would let the village cows stray into his meadows, then horses from the night pasture would get among his corn. Pahom turned them out again and again, and forgave their owners, and for a long time he forbore to prosecute anyone. But at last he lost patience and complained to the District Court. He knew it was the peasants' want of land, and no evil intent on their part, that caused the trouble, but he thought:

"I can't go on overlooking it, or they'll destroy all I have. They must be taught a lesson."

So he had them up, gave them one lesson, and then another, and two or three of the peasants were fined. After a time Pahom's neighbours began to bear him a grudge for this, and would now and then let their cattle on to his land on purpose. One peasant even got into Pahom's wood at night and cut down five young lime trees for their bark. Pahom, passing through the wood one day, noticed something white. He came nearer and saw the stripped trunks lying on the ground, and close by stood the stumps where the trees had been. Pahom was furious.

"If he'd only cut one here and there it would have been bad enough," thought Pahom, "but the rascal has actually cut down a whole clump. If I could only find out who did this, I'd get even with him."

He racked his brains as to who it could be. Finally he decided: "It must be Simon—no one else could have done it." So he went to Simon's homestead to have a look around, but he found nothing, and only had an angry scene. However, he now felt more certain than ever that Simon had done it, and he lodged a complaint. Simon was summoned. The case was tried, and retried, and at the end of it all Simon was acquitted, there being no evidence against him. Pahom felt still more aggrieved, and let his anger loose upon the Elder and the Judges.

"You let thieves grease your palms," said he. "If you were honest folk yourselves you wouldn't let a thief go free."

So Pahom quarrelled with the judges and with his neighbours. Threats to burn his hut began to be uttered. So though Pahom had more land, his place in the community was much worse than before.

About this time a rumour got about that many people were moving to new parts.

"There's no need for me to leave my land," thought Pahom. "But some of the others may leave our village and then there'd be more room for us. I'd take over their land myself and make my estate somewhat bigger. I could then live more at ease. As it is, I'm still too cramped to be comfortable."

One day Pahom was sitting at home, when a peasant, passing through the village, happened to drop in. He was allowed to stay the night, and supper was given him. Pahom had a talk with this peasant and asked him where he came from. The stranger answered that he came from beyond the Volga, where he had been working. One word led to another, and the man went on to say that many people were settling in those parts. He told how some people from his village had settled there. They had joined the community there and had had twenty-five acres per man granted them. The land was so good, he said, that the rye sown on it grew as high as a horse, and so thick that five cuts of a sickle made a sheaf. One peasant, he said, had brought nothing with him but his bare hands, and now he had six horses and two cows of his own.

Pahom's heart kindled with desire.

"Why should I suffer in this narrow hole, if one can live so well elsewhere?" he thought. "I'll sell my land and my homestead here, and with the money I'll start afresh over there and get everything new. In this crowded place one is always having trouble. But I must first go and find out all about it myself."

Toward summer he got ready and started out. He went down the Volga on a steamer to Samara, then walked another three hundred miles on foot, and at last reached the place. It was just as the stranger had said. The peasants had plenty of land: every man had twenty-five acres of communal land given him for his use, and anyone who had money could buy, besides, at a ruble-and-a-half an acre, as much good freehold land as he wanted.

Having found out all he wished to know, Pahom returned home as autumn came on, and began selling off his belongings. He sold his land at a profit, sold his homestead and all his cattle, and withdrew from membership in the village. He only waited till the spring, and then started with his family for the new settlement.

IV

As soon as Pahom and his family reached their new abode, he applied for admission into the Council of a large village. He stood treat to the Elders and obtained the necessary documents. Five shares of communal land were given him for his own and his sons' use: that is to say—125 acres (not all together, but in different fields) besides the use of the communal pasture. Pahom put up the buildings he needed and bought cattle. Of the communal land alone he had three times as much as at his former home, and the land was good wheat-land. He was ten times better off than he had been. He had plenty of arable land and pasturage, and could keep as many head of cattle as he liked.

At first, in the bustle of building and settling down, Pahom was pleased with it all, but when he got used to it he began to think that even here he hadn't enough land. The first year he sowed wheat on his share of the communal land and had a good crop. He wanted to go on sowing wheat, but had not enough communal land for the purpose, and what he had already used was not available, for in those parts wheat is sown only on virgin soil or on fallow land. It is sown for one or two years, and then the land lies fallow till it is again overgrown with steppe grass. There were many who wanted such land, and there was not enough for all, so that people quarrelled about it. Those who were better off wanted it for growing wheat, and those who were poor wanted it to let to dealers, so that they might raise money to pay their taxes. Pahom wanted to sow more wheat, so he rented land from a dealer for a year. He sowed much wheat and had a fine crop, but the land was too far from the village—the wheat had to be carted more than ten miles. After a time Pahom noticed that some peasant-dealers were living on separate farms and were growing wealthy, and he thought:

"If I were to buy some freehold land and have a homestead on it, it would be a different thing altogether. Then it would all be fine and close together."

The question of buying freehold land recurred to him again and again.

He went on in the same way for three years, renting land and sowing wheat. The seasons turned out well and the crops were good, so that he began to lay by money. He might have gone on living contentedly, but he grew tired of having to rent other people's land every year, and having to scramble for it. Wherever there was good land to be had, the peasants would rush for it and it was taken up at once, so that unless you were sharp about it you got none. It happened in the third year that he and a dealer together rented a piece of pasture land from some peasants, and they had already ploughed it up, when there was some dispute and the peasants went to law about it, and things fell out so that the labour was all lost.

"If it were my own land," thought Pahom, "I should be independent, and there wouldn't be all this unpleasantness."

So Pahom began looking out for land which he could buy, and he came across a peasant who had bought thirteen hundred acres, but having got into difficulties was willing to sell again cheap. Pahom bargained and haggled with him, and at last they settled the price at fifteen hundred rubles, part in cash and part to be paid later. They had all but clinched the matter when a passing dealer happened to stop at Pahom's one day to get feed for his horses. He drank tea with Pahom, and they had a talk. The dealer said that he was returning from the land of the Bashkirs, far away, where he had bought thirteen

thousand acres of land, all for a thousand rubles. Pahom questioned him further, and the dealer said:

"All one has to do is to make friends with the chiefs. I gave away about one hundred rubles' worth of silk robes and carpets, besides a case of tea, and I gave wine to those who would drink it; and I got the land for less than three kopecks an acre." And he showed Pahom the title deed, saying:

"The land lies near a river, and the whole steppe is virgin soil."

Pahom plied him with questions, and the dealer said:

"There's more land there than you could cover if you walked a year, and it all belongs to the Bashkirs. They're as simple as sheep, and land can be got almost for nothing."

"There, now," thought Pahom, "with my one thousand rubles, why should I get only thirteen hundred acres, and saddle myself with a debt besides? If I take it out there, I can get more than ten times as much for my money."

V

Pahom inquired how to get to the place, and as soon as the grain dealer had left him, he prepared to go there himself. He left his wife to look after the homestead, and started on his journey, taking his hired man with him. They stopped at a town on their way and bought a case of tea, some wine, and other presents, as the grain dealer had advised.

On and on they went until they had gone more than three hundred miles, and on the seventh day they came to a place where the Bashkirs had pitched their round tents. It was all just as the dealer had said. The people lived on the steppe, by a river, in felt-covered tents. They neither tilled the ground nor ate bread. Their cattle and horses grazed in herds on the steppe. The colts were tethered behind the tents, and the mares were driven to them twice a day. The mares were milked, and from the milk kumiss was made. It was the women who prepared the kumiss, and they also made cheese. As far as the men were concerned, drinking kumiss and tea, eating mutton, and playing on their pipes was all they cared about. They were all stout and merry, and all the summer long they never thought of doing any work. They were quite ignorant, and knew no Russian, but were good-natured enough.

As soon as they saw Pahom, they came out of their tents and gathered around their visitor. An interpreter was found, and Pahom told them he had come about some land. The Bashkirs seemed very glad; they took Pahom and led him into one of the best tents, where they made him sit on some down cushions placed on a carpet, while they sat around him. They gave him some tea and kumiss, and had a sheep killed, and gave him mutton to eat. Pahom took presents out of his cart and distributed them among the Bashkirs, and divided the tea amongst them. The Bashkirs were delighted. They talked a great deal among themselves, and then told the interpreter what to say.

"They wish to tell you," said the interpreter, "that they like you, and that it's our custom to do all we can to please a guest and to repay him for his gifts. You have given us presents, now tell us which of the things we possess please you best, that we may present them to you."

"What pleases me best here," answered Pahom, "is your land. Our land is crowded and the soil is worn out, but you have plenty of land, and it is good land. I never saw the likes of it."

The interpreter told the Bashkirs what Pahom had said. They talked among themselves for a while. Pahom could not understand what they were saying, but saw that they were much amused and heard them shout and laugh. Then they were silent and looked at Pahom while the interpreter said:

"They wish me to tell you that in return for your presents they will gladly give you as much land as you want. You have only to point it out with your hand and it is yours."

The Bashkirs talked again for a while and began to dispute. Pahom asked what they were disputing about, and the interpreter told him that some of them thought they ought to ask their Chief about the land and not act in his absence, while others thought there was no need to wait for his return.

VI

While the Bashkirs were disputing, a man in a large fox-fur cap appeared on the scene. They all became silent and rose to their feet. The interpreter said: "This is our Chief himself."

Pahom immediately fetched the best dressing gown and five pounds of tea, and offered these to the Chief. The Chief accepted them, and seated himself in the place of honour. The Bashkirs at once began telling him something. The Chief listened for a while, then made a sign with his head for them to be silent, and addressing himself to Pahom, said in Russian:

"Well, so be it. Choose whatever piece of land you like; we have plenty of it."

"How can I take as much as I like?" thought Pahom. "I must get a deed to make it secure, or else they may say: 'It is yours,' and afterward may take it away again."

"Thank you for your kind words," he said aloud. "You have much land, and I only want a little. But I should like to be sure which portion is mine. Could it not be measured and made over to me? Life and death are in God's hands. You good people give it to me, but your children might wish to take it back again."

"You are quite right," said the Chief. "We will make it over to you."

"I heard that a dealer had been here," continued Pahom, "and that you gave him a little land, too, and signed title deeds to that effect. I should like to have it done in the same way."

The Chief understood.

"Yes," replied he, "that can be done quite easily. We have a scribe, and we will go to town with you and have the deed properly sealed."

"And what will be the price?" asked Pahom.

"Our price is always the same: one thousand rubles a day."

Pahom did not understand.

"A day? What measure is that? How many acres would that be?"

"We do not know how to reckon it out," said the Chief. "We sell it by the day. As much as you can go around on your feet in a day is yours, and the price is one thousand rubles a day."

Pahom was surprised.

"But in a day you can get around a large tract of land," he said.

The Chief laughed.

"It will all be yours!" said he. "But there is one condition: If you don't return on the same day to the spot whence you started, your money is lost."

"But how am I to mark the way that I have gone?"

"Why, we shall go to any spot you like, and stay there. You must start from that spot and make your round, taking a spade with you. Wherever you think necessary, make a mark. At every turning, dig a hole and pile up the turf; then afterward we will go around with a plough from hole to hole. You may make as large a circuit as you please, but before the sun sets you must return to the place you started from. All the land you cover will be yours."

Pahom was delighted. It was decided to start early next morning. They talked a while, and after drinking some more kumiss and eating some more mutton, they had tea again, and then the night came on. They gave Pahom a feather bed to sleep on, and the Bashkirs dispersed for the night, promising to assemble the next morning at daybreak and ride out before sunrise to the appointed spot.

VII

Pahom lay on the feather bed, but could not sleep. He kept thinking about the land.

"What a large tract I'll mark off!" thought he. "I can easily do thirty-five miles in a day. The days are long now, and within a circuit of thirty-five miles what a lot of land there will be! I'll sell the poorer land, or let it to peasants, but I'll pick out the best and farm it myself. I'll buy two ox teams and hire two more labourers. About a hundred and fifty acres shall be ploughland, and I'll pasture cattle on the rest."

Pahom lay awake all night, and dozed off only just before dawn. Hardly were his eyes closed when he had a dream. He thought he was lying in that same tent and heard somebody chuckling outside. He wondered who it could be, and rose and went out, and he saw the Bashkir Chief sitting in front of the tent holding his sides and rolling about with laughter. Going nearer to the Chief, Pahom asked: "What are you laughing at?" But he saw that it was no longer the Chief, but the grain dealer who had recently stopped at his house and had told him about the land. Just as Pahom was going to ask: "Have you been here long?" he saw that it was not the dealer, but the peasant who had come up from the Volga, long ago, to Pahom's old home. Then he saw that it was not the peasant either, but the Devil himself with hoofs and horns, sitting there and chuckling, and before him lay a man, prostrate on the ground, barefooted, with only trousers and a shirt on. And Pahom dreamed that he looked more attentively to see what sort of man it was lying there, and he saw that the man was dead, and that it was himself. Horror-struck, he awoke.

"What things one dreams about!" thought he.

Looking around he saw through the open door that the dawn was breaking.

"It's time to wake them up," thought he. "We ought to be starting."

He got up, roused his man (who was sleeping in his cart), bade him harness, and went to call the Bashkirs.

"It's time to go to the steppe to measure the land," he said.

The Bashkirs rose and assembled, and the Chief came, too. Then they began drinking kumiss again, and offered Pahom some tea, but he would not wait.

"If we are to go, let's go. It's high time," said he.

VIII

The Bashkirs got ready and they all started: some mounted on horses and some in carts. Pahom drove in his own small cart with his servant and took a spade with him. When they reached the steppe, the red dawn was beginning to kindle. They ascended a hillock (called by the Bashkirs a *shikhan*) and, dismounting from their carts and their horses, gathered in one spot. The Chief came up to Pahom and, stretching out his arm toward the plain:

"See," said he, "all this, as far as your eye can reach, is ours. You may have any part of it you like."

Pahom's eyes glistened: it was all virgin soil, as flat as the palm of your hand, as black as the seed of a poppy, and in the hollows different kinds of grasses grew breast-high.

The Chief took off his fox-fur cap, placed it on the ground, and said:

"This will be the mark. Start from here, and return here again. All the land you go around shall be yours."

Pahom took out his money and put it on the cap. Then he took off his outer coat, remaining in his sleeveless undercoat. He unfastened his girdle and tied it tight below his stomach, put a little bag of bread into the breast of his coat, and, tying a flask of water to his girdle, he drew up the tops of his boots, took the spade from his man, and stood ready to start. He considered for some moments which way he had better go—it was tempting everywhere.

"No matter," he concluded, "I'll go toward the rising sun."

He turned his face to the east, stretched himself, and waited for the sun to appear above the rim.

"I must lose no time," he thought, "and it's easier walking while it's still cool."

The sun's rays had hardly flashed above the horizon when Pahom, carrying the spade over his shoulder, went down into the steppe.

Pahom started walking neither slowly nor quickly. After having gone a thousand yards he stopped, dug a hole, and placed pieces of turf one on another to make it more visible. Then he went on; and now that he had walked off his stiffness he quickened his pace. After a while he dug another hole.

Pahom looked back. The hillock could be distinctly seen in the sunlight, with the people on it, and the glittering iron rims of the cartwheels. At a rough guess Pahom concluded that he had walked three miles. It was growing warmer; he took off his undercoat, slung it across his shoulder, and went on again. It had grown quite warm now; he looked at the sun—it was time to think of breakfast.

"The first shift is done, but there are four in a day, and it's too soon yet to turn. But I'll just take off my boots," said he to himself.

He sat down, took off his boots, stuck them into his girdle, and went on. It was easy walking now.

"I'll go on for another three miles," thought he, "and then turn to the left. This spot is so fine that it would be a pity to lose it. The further one goes, the better the land seems."

He went straight on for a while, and when he looked around, the hillock was scarcely visible and the people on it looked like black ants, and he could just see something glistening there in the sun.

"Ah," thought Pahom, "I have gone far enough in this direction; it's time to turn. Besides, I'm in a regular sweat, and very thirsty."

He stopped, dug a large hole, and heaped up pieces of turf. Next he untied his flask, had a drink, and then turned sharply to the left. He went on and on; the grass was high, and it was very hot.

Pahom began to grow tired: he looked at the sun and saw that it was noon.

"Well," he thought, "I must have a rest."

He sat down, and ate some bread and drank some water; but he did not lie down, thinking that if he did he might fall asleep. After sitting a little while, he went on again. At first he walked easily; the food had strengthened him; but it had become terribly hot and he felt sleepy. Still he went on, thinking: "An hour to suffer, a lifetime to live."

He went a long way in this direction also, and was about to turn to the left again, when he perceived a damp hollow: "It would be a pity to leave that out," he thought. "Flax would do well there." So he went on past the hollow and dug a hole on the other side of it before he made a sharp turn. Pahom looked toward the hillock. The heat made the air hazy: it seemed to be quivering, and through the haze the people on the hillock could scarcely be seen.

"Ah," thought Pahom, "I have made the sides too long; I must make this one shorter." And he went along the third side, stepping faster. He looked at the sun: it was nearly halfway to the horizon, and he had not yet done two miles of the third side of the square. He was still ten miles from the goal.

"No," he thought, "though it will make my land lopsided, I must hurry back in a straight line now. I might go too far, and as it is I have a great deal of land."

So Pahom hurriedly dug a hole and turned straight toward the hillock.

IX

Pahom went straight toward the hillock, but he now walked with difficulty. He was exhausted from the heat, his bare feet were cut and bruised, and his legs began to fail. He longed to rest, but it was impossible if he meant to get back before sunset. The sun waits for no man, and it was sinking lower and lower.

"Oh, Lord," he thought, "if only I have not blundered trying for too much! What if I am too late?"

He looked toward the hillock and at the sun. He was still far from his goal, and the sun was already near the rim of the sky.

Pahom walked on and on; it was very hard walking, but he went quicker and quicker. He pressed on, but was still far from the place. He began running, threw away his coat, his boots, his flask, and his cap, and kept only the spade which he used as a support.

"What am I to do?" he thought again. "I've grasped too much and ruined the whole affair. I can't get there before the sun sets."

And this fear made him still more breathless. Pahom kept on running; his soaking shirt and trousers stuck to him, and his mouth was parched. His breast was working like a blacksmith's bellows, his heart was beating like a hammer, and his legs were giving way as if they did not belong to him. Pahom was seized with terror lest he should die of the strain.

Though afraid of death, he could not stop.

"After having run all that way they will call me a fool if I stop now," thought he.

And he ran on and on, and drew near and heard the Bashkirs yelling and shouting to him, and their cries inflamed his heart still more. He gathered his last strength and ran on.

The sun was close to the rim of the sky and, cloaked in mist, looked large, and red as blood. Now, yes, now it was about to set! The sun was quite low, but he was also quite near his goal. Pahom could already see the people on the hillock waving their arms to make him hurry. He could see the fox-fur cap on the ground and the money in it, and the Chief sitting on the ground holding his sides. And Pahom remembered his dream.

"There's plenty of land," thought he, "but will God let me live on it? I have lost my life, I have lost my life! Never will I reach that spot!"

Pahom looked at the sun, which had reached the earth: one side of it had already disappeared. With all his remaining strength he rushed on, bending his body forward so that his legs could hardly follow fast enough to keep him from falling. Just as he reached the hillock it suddenly grew dark. He looked up—the sun had already set!

He gave a cry: "All my labour has been in vain," thought he, and was about to stop, but he could hear the Bashkirs still shouting, and remembered that though to him, from below, the sun seemed to have set, they on the hillock could still see it. He took a long breath and ran up the hillock. It was still light there. He reached the top and saw the cap. Before it sat the Chief, laughing and holding his sides. Again Pahom remembered his dream, and he uttered a cry: his legs gave way beneath him, he fell forward and reached the cap with his hands.

"Ah, that's a fine fellow!" exclaimed the Chief. "He has gained much land!"

Pahom's servant came running up and tried to raise him, but he saw that blood was flowing from his mouth. Pahom was dead.

The Bashkirs clicked their tongues to show their pity.

His servant picked up the spade and dug a grave long enough for Pahom to lie in, and buried him in it.

Six feet from his head to his heels was all he needed.

Questions

1 (a) What are the various advantages and disadvantages of the city and country presented in Part I?

(b) Which of the two lifestyles would you prefer?

2 What reasons did Pahom give for wanting to buy the land that was for sale? (Part II)

3 What changes do we see in Pahom in Parts III and IV? Refer to specific incidents or statements in your answer.

4 What indications are there in the story that the Bashkirs knew what might happen to Pahom? (Parts VI and VII)

5 Explain the proverbs *Loss and gain are brothers twain* (page 109) and *An hour to suffer, a lifetime to live* (page 121).

6 What answers to the question asked in the title of this story would be given by:

(a) Pahom?

(b) the Bashkirs?

(c) Tolstoy?

(d) you?

Give reasons for your answers.

Writing

Write a story that answers one of these questions:

• How much money does a person (man/woman/child/Australian) need?

• How much power does a car need?

• How much education does a person need?

• Did you really have to tell me that?

Leo Tolstoy

Notes

page 110   *Pahom . . . was lying on the top of the stove:* a very large stove used for room heating. These were common in eastern and central Europe, and frequently had beds built over them.

page 111   *ruble:* Russian unit of money, nowadays usually spelt "rouble".

page 113   *Volga:* the largest river in European Russia, travelling from north to south into the Caspian Sea. It was (and still is) a major transport route.

Samara: A city on the Volga, south east of Moscow. Its modern-day name is Kuybyshev.

page 114   *the land of the Bashkirs:* an area in the south west Urals, (the mountains that form the dividing line between Russia and Siberia).

page 116   *less than three kopecks an acre:* 100 kopecks equal one rouble. Less than three kopecks an acre would be very cheap land indeed, (perhaps a cent per acre).

kumiss: also spelt "koumis". As koumis is a fermented drink it would also contain alcohol. It is sometimes distilled to make a stronger drink, which is also known as koumis.

page 117   *pounds:* there are approximately 2.2 pounds in a kilogram.

H. G. Wells
The Truth About Pyecraft

Herbert George Wells (1866-1946) began his working life as a shop assistant. He later studied science, which shows in many of his short stories and also in his popular novels *The Time Machine, The Invisible Man* and *The War of the Worlds*. His novels on social problems are highly regarded. He wrote many books on political, historical and philosophical issues of his time.

H E sits not a dozen yards away. If I glance over my shoulder I can see him. And if I catch his eye—and usually I catch his eye—it meets me with an expression—

It is mainly an imploring look—and yet with suspicion in it.

Confound his suspicion! If I wanted to tell on him I should have told long ago. I don't tell and I won't tell, and he ought to feel at his ease. As if anything so gross and fat as he could feel at ease! Who would believe me if I did tell?

Poor old Pyecraft! Great, uneasy jelly of substance! The fattest clubman in London.

He sits at one of the little club tables in the huge bay by the fire, stuffing. What is he stuffing? I glance judiciously and catch him biting at a round of hot buttered teacake, with his eyes on me. Confound him!—with his eyes on me!

That settles it, Pyecraft! Since you *will* be abject, since you *will* behave as though I was not a man of honour, here, right under your embedded eyes, I write the thing down—the plain truth about Pyecraft. The man I helped, the man I shielded, and who has requited me by making my club unendurable, absolutely unendurable, with his liquid appeal, with the perpetual "don't tell" of his looks.

And, besides, why does he keep on eternally eating?

Well, here goes for the truth, the whole truth, and nothing but the truth!

Pyecraft—I made the acquaintance of Pyecraft in this very smoking-room. I was a young, nervous new member, and he saw it. I was sitting all alone, wishing I knew more of the members, and suddenly he came, a great rolling front of chins and abdomina, towards me, and grunted and sat down in a chair close by me and wheezed for a space, and scraped for a space with a match and lit a cigar, and then addressed me. I forget what he said—something about the matches not lighting properly, and afterwards as he talked he kept stopping the waiters one by one as they went by, and telling them about the matches in that thin, fluty voice he has. But, anyhow, it was in some such way we began our talking.

He talked about various things and came round to games. And thence to my figure and complexion. "You ought to be a good cricketer," he said. I suppose I am slender, slender to what some people would call lean, and I suppose I am rather dark, still—I am not ashamed of having a Hindu great-grandmother, but, for all that, I don't want casual strangers to see through me at a glance to *her.* So that I was set against Pyecraft from the beginning.

But he only talked about me in order to get to himself.

"I expect," he said, "you take no more exercise than I do, and probably you eat no less." (Like all excessively obese people he fancied he ate nothing.) "Yet"—and he smiled an oblique smile—"we differ."

And then he began to talk about his fatness and his fatness; all he did for his fatness and all he was going to do for his fatness; what people had advised him to do for his fatness and what he had heard of people doing for fatness similar to his. *"A priori,"* he said, "one would think a question of nutrition could be answered by dietary and a question of assimilation by drugs." It was stifling. It was dumpling talk. It made me feel swelled to hear him.

One stands that sort of thing once in a way at a club, but a time came when I fancied I was standing too much. He took to me altogether too conspicuously. I could never go into the smoking-room but he would come wallowing towards me, and sometimes he came and gormandised round and about me while I had my lunch. He seemed at times almost to be clinging to me. He was a bore, but not so fearful a bore as to be limited to me; and from the first there was something in his manner—almost as though he knew, almost as though he penetrated to the fact that I *might*—that there was a remote, exceptional chance in me that no one else presented.

"I'd give anything to get it down," he would say—"anything," and peer at me over his vast cheeks and pant.

Poor old Pyecraft! He has just gonged, no doubt to order another buttered teacake!

He came to the actual thing one day. "Our Pharmacopœia," he said, "our Western Pharmacopœia, is anything but the last word of medical science. In the East, I've been told—"

He stopped and stared at me. It was like being at an aquarium.

I was quite suddenly angry with him. "Look here," I said, "who told you about my great-grandmother's recipes?"

"Well," he fenced.

"Every time we've met for a week," I said—"and we've met pretty often—you've given me a broad hint or so about that little secret of mine."

"Well," he said, "now the cat's out of the bag, I'll admit, yes, it is so. I had it—"

"From Pattison?"

"Indirectly," he said, which I believe was lying, "yes."

"Pattison," I said, "took that stuff at his own risk."

He pursed his mouth and bowed.

"My great-grandmother's recipes," I said, "are queer things to handle. My father was near making me promise—"

"He didn't?"

"No. But he warned me. He himself used one—once."

"Ah! . . . But do you think—? Suppose—suppose there did happen to be one—"

"The things are curious documents," I said. "Even the smell of 'em . . . No!"

But after going so far Pyecraft was resolved I should go farther. I was always a little afraid if I tried his patience too much he would fall on me suddenly and smother me. I own I was weak. But I was also annoyed with Pyecraft. I had got to that state of feeling for him that disposed me to say, "Well, *take* the risk!" The little affair of Pattison to which I have alluded was a different matter altogether. What it was doesn't concern us now, but I knew, anyhow, that the particular recipe I used then was safe. The rest I didn't know so much about, and, on the whole, I was inclined to doubt their safety pretty completely.

Yet even if Pyecraft got poisoned—

I must confess the poisoning of Pyecraft struck me as an immense undertaking.

That evening I took that queer, odd-scented sandalwood box out of my safe and turned the rustling skins over. The gentleman who wrote the recipes for my great-grandmother evidently had a weakness for skins of a miscellaneous origin, and his handwriting was cramped to the last degree. Some of the things are quite unreadable to me—though my family, with its Indian Civil Service associations, has kept up a knowledge of Hindustani from generation to generation—and none are absolutely plain sailing. But I found the one that I knew was there soon enough, and sat on the floor by my safe for some time looking at it.

"Look here," said I to Pyecraft next day, and snatched the slip away from his eager grasp.

"So far as I can make out, this is a recipe for Loss of Weight. ("Ah!" said Pyecraft.) I'm not absolutely sure, but I think it's that. And if you take my advice you'll leave it alone. Because, you know—I blacken my blood in your interest, Pyecraft—my ancestors on that side were, so far as I can gather, a jolly queer lot. See?"

"Let me try it," said Pyecraft.

I leant back in my chair. My imagination made one mighty effort and fell flat within me. "What in heaven's name, Pyecraft," I asked, "do you think you'll look like when you get thin?"

He was impervious to reason. I made him promise never to say a word to me about his disgusting fatness again whatever happened—never, and then I handed him that little piece of skin.

"It's nasty stuff," I said.

"No matter," he said, and took it.

He goggled at it. "But—but—" he said.

He had just discovered that it wasn't English.

"To the best of my ability," I said, "I will do you a translation."

I did my best. After that we didn't speak for a fortnight. Whenever he approached me I frowned and motioned him away, and he respected our compact, but at the end of the fortnight he was as fat as ever. And then he got a word in.

"I must speak," he said. "It isn't fair. There's something wrong. It's done me no good. You're not doing your great-grandmother justice."

"Where's the recipe?"

He produced it gingerly from his pocket-book.

I ran my eye over the items. "Was the egg addled?" I asked.

"No. Ought it to have been?"

"That," I said, "goes without saying in all my poor dear great-grandmother's recipes. When condition or quality is not specified you must get the worst. She was drastic or nothing . . . And there's one or two possible alternatives to some of these other things. You got *fresh* rattlesnake venom?"

"I got a rattlesnake from Jamrach's. It cost—it cost—"

"That's your affair, anyhow. This last item—"

"I know a man who—"

"Yes. H'm. Well, I'll write the alternatives down. So far as I know the language, the spelling of this recipe is particularly atrocious. By-the-bye, dog here probably means pariah dog."

For a month after that I saw Pyecraft constantly at the club and as fat and anxious as ever. He kept our treaty, but at times he broke the spirit of it by shaking his head despondently. Then one day in the cloak-room he said, "Your great-grandmother—"

"Not a word against her," I said; and he held his peace.

I could have fancied he had desisted, and I saw him one day talking to three new members about his fatness as though he was in search of other recipes. And then, quite unexpectedly his telegram came.

"Mr Formalyn!" bawled a page-boy under my nose and I took the telegram and opened it at once.

"*For Heaven's sake come.—Pyecraft.*"

"H'm," said I, and to tell the truth I was so pleased at the rehabilitation of my great-grandmother's reputation this evidently promised that I made a most excellent lunch.

I got Pyecraft's address from the hall porter. Pyecraft inhabited the upper half of a house in Bloomsbury, and I went there so soon as I had done my coffee and Trappistine. I did not wait to finish my cigar.

"Mr Pyecraft?" said I, at the front door.

They believed he was ill; he hadn't been out for two days.

"He expects me," said I, and they sent me up.

I rang the bell at the lattice-door upon the landing.

"He shouldn't have tried it, anyhow," I said to myself. "A man who eats like a pig ought to look like a pig."

An obviously worthy woman, with an anxious face and a carelessly placed cap, came and surveyed me through the lattice.

I gave my name and she opened his door for me in a dubious fashion.

"Well?" said I, as we stood together inside Pyecraft's piece of the landing.

" 'E said you was to come in if you came," she said, and regarded me, making no motion to show me anywhere. And then, confidentially, " 'E's locked in, sir."

"Locked in?"

"Locked himself in yesterday morning and 'asn't let anyone in since, sir. And ever and again *swearing.* Oh, my!"

I stared at the door she indicated by her glances. "In there?" I said.

"Yes, sir."

"What's up?"

She shook her head sadly. " 'E keeps on calling for vittles, sir. '*Eavy* vittles 'e wants. I get 'im what I can. Pork 'e's 'ad, sooit puddin', sossiges, noo bread. Everythink like that. Left outside, if you please, and me go away. 'E's eatin', sir somethink *awful.*"

There came a piping bawl from inside the door: "That Formalyn?"

"That you Pyecraft?" I shouted, and went and banged the door.

"Tell her to go away."

I did.

Then I could hear a curious pattering upon the door, almost like someone feeling for the handle in the dark, and Pyecraft's familiar grunts.

"It's all right," I said, "she's gone."

But for a long time the door didn't open.

I heard the key turn. Then Pyecraft's voice said, "Come in."

I turned the handle and opened the door. Naturally I expected to see Pyecraft.

Well, you know, he wasn't there!

I never had such a shock in my life. There was his sitting-room in a state of untidy disorder, plates and dishes among the books and writing things, and several chairs overturned, but Pyecraft—

"It's all right, ol' man; shut the door," he said, and then I discovered him.

There he was right up close to the cornice in the corner by the door, as though someone had glued him to the ceiling. His face was anxious and angry. He panted and gesticulated. "Shut the door," he said. "If that woman gets hold of it—"

I shut the door, and went and stood away from him and stared.

"If anything gives way and you tumble down," I said, "you'll break your neck, Pyecraft."

"I wish I could," he wheezed.

"A man of your age and weight getting up to kiddish gymnastics—"

"Don't," he said, and looked agonised. "Your damned great-grandmother—"

"Be careful," I warned him.

"I'll tell you," he said, and gesticulated.

"How the deuce," said I, "are you holding on up there?"

And then abruptly I realised that he was not holding on at all, that he was floating up there—just as a gas-filled bladder might have floated in the same position. He began a struggle to thrust himself away from the ceiling and to clamber down the wall to me. "It's that prescription," he panted, as he did so. "Your great-gran—"

"*No!*" I cried.

He took hold of a framed engraving rather carelessly as he spoke and it gave way, and he flew back to the ceiling again, while the picture smashed on to the sofa. Bump he went against the ceiling, and I knew then why he was all over white on the more salient curves and angles of his person. He tried again more carefully, coming down by way of the mantel.

It was really a most extraordinary spectacle, that great, fat apoplectic-looking man upside down and trying to get from the ceiling to the floor. "That prescription," he said. "Too successful."

"How?"

"Loss of weight—almost complete."

And then, of course, I understood.

"By Jove, Pyecraft," said I, "what you wanted was a cure for fatness! But you always called it weight. You would call it weight."

Somehow I was extremely delighted. I quite liked Pyecraft for the time. "Let me help you!" I said, and took his hand and pulled him down. He kicked about, trying to get foothold somewhere. It was very like holding a flag on a windy day.

"That table," he said, pointing, "is solid mahogany and very heavy. If you can put me under that—"

I did, and there he wallowed about like a captive balloon, while I stood on his hearthrug and talked to him.

I lit a cigar. "Tell me," I said, "what happened?"

"I took it," he said.

"How did it taste?"

"Oh, *beastly!*"

I should fancy they all did. Whether one regards the ingredients or the probable compound or the possible results, almost all my great-grandmother's remedies appear to me at least to be extraordinarily uninviting. For my own part—

"I took a little sip first."

"Yes?"

"And as I felt lighter and better after an hour, I decided to take the draught."

"My dear Pyecraft!"

"I held my nose," he explained. "And then I kept on getting lighter and lighter—and helpless, you know."

He gave way suddenly to a burst of passion. "What the goodness am I to *do*?" he said.

"There's one thing pretty evident," I said, "that you mustn't do. If you go out of doors you'll go up and up." I waved an arm upward. "They'd have to send Santos-Dumont after you to bring you down again."

"I suppose it will wear off?"

I shook my head. "I don't think you can count on that," I said.

And then there was another burst of passion, and he kicked out at adjacent chairs and banged the floor. He behaved just as I should have expected a great, fat, self-indulgent man to behave under trying circumstances—that is to say, very badly. He spoke of me and of my great-grandmother with an utter want of discretion.

"I never asked you to take the stuff," I said.

And generously disregarding the insults he was putting upon me, I sat down in his armchair and began to talk to him in a sober, friendly fashion.

I pointed out to him that this was a trouble he had brought upon himself, and that it had almost an air of poetical justice. He had eaten too much. This he disputed, and for a time we argued the point. He became noisy and violent, so I desisted from this aspect of his lesson. "And then," said I, "you committed the sin of euphemism. You called it, not Fat, which is just and inglorious, but Weight. You—"

He interrupted to say that he recognised all that. What was he to *do?*

I suggested that he should adapt himself to his new conditions. So we came to the really sensible part of the business. I suggested that it would not be difficult for him to learn to walk about on the ceiling with his hands—

"I can't sleep," he said.

But that was no great difficulty. It was quite possible, I pointed out, to make a shake-up under a wire mattress, fasten the under things on with tapes, and have a blanket, sheet, and coverlet to button at the side. He would have to confide in his housekeeper, I said; and after some squabbling he agreed to that. (Afterwards it was quite delightful to see the beautifully matter-of-fact way with which the good lady took all these amazing inversions.) He could have a library ladder in his room, and all his meals could be laid on the top of his bookcase. We also hit on an ingenious device by which he could get to the floor whenever he wanted, which was simply to put the *British Encyclopædia* (tenth edition) on the top of his open shelves. He just pulled out a couple of volumes and held on, and down he came. And we agreed there must be iron staples along the skirting, so that he could cling to those whenever he wanted to get about the room on the lower level.

As we got on with the thing I found myself almost keenly interested. It was I who called in the housekeeper and broke matters to her, and it was I chiefly who fixed up the inverted bed. In fact, I spent two whole days at his flat. I am a handy, interfering sort of man with a screwdriver, and I made all sorts of ingenious adaptations for him— ran a wire to bring his bells within reach, turned all his electric lights up instead of down, and so on. The whole affair was extremely curious and interesting to me, and it was delightful to think of Pyecraft like some great, fat blow-fly, crawling about on his ceiling and clambering round the lintel of his doors from one room to another, and never, never, never coming to the club any more . . .

Then, you know, my fatal ingenuity got the better of me. I was sitting by his fire drinking his whisky, and he was up in his favourite corner by the cornice, tacking a Turkey carpet to the ceiling, when the idea struck me. "By Jove, Pyecraft!" I said, "all this is totally unnecessary."

And before I could calculate the complete consequences of my notion I blurted it out. "Lead underclothing," said I, and the mischief was done.

Pyecraft received the thing almost in tears. "To be right ways up again—" he said.

I gave him the whole secret before I saw where it would take me. "Buy sheet lead," I said, "stamp it into discs. Sew 'em all over your underclothes until you have enough. Have lead-soled boots, carry a bag of solid lead, and the thing is done! Instead of being a prisoner here you may go abroad again, Pyecraft; you may travel—"

A still happier idea came to me. "You need never fear a shipwreck. All you need do is just slip off some or all of your clothes, take the necessary amount of luggage in your hand, and float up in the air—"

In his emotion he dropped the tack-hammer within an ace of my head. "By Jove!" he said, "I shall be able to go back to the club again."

The thing pulled me up short. "By Jove!" I said, faintly. "Yes. Of course—you will."

He did. He does. There he sits behind me now, stuffing—as I live!— a third go of buttered tea-cake. And no one in the whole world knows— except his housekeeper and me—that he weighs practically nothing; that he is a mere boring mass of assimilatory matter, mere clouds in clothing, *niente, nefas*, the most inconsiderable of men. There he sits watching until I have done this writing. Then, if he can, he will waylay me. He will come billowing up to me . . .

He will tell me over again all about it, how it feels, how it doesn't feel, how he sometimes hopes it is passing off a little. And always somewhere in that fat, abundant discourse he will say, "The secret's keeping, eh? If anyone knew of it— I should be so ashamed. . . . Makes a fellow look such a fool, you know. Crawling about on a ceiling and all that . . . "

And now to elude Pyecraft, occupying, as he does, an admirable strategic position between me and the door.

❖

Questions

1 The introduction to this story whets the reader's appetite by presenting an extraordinary figure, and suggesting that there is a story to be told about him. Which of the narrator's statements made you wonder what "the truth about Pyecraft" might be?

2 What do the names Formalyn (*formalin*) and Pyecraft (*pie craft*) suggest about the characters?
3 There are examples of racial prejudice in this story. Where?
4 Formalyn suggests some ways in which Pyecraft could modify his surroundings to enable him to live relatively normally (page 133). What other adjustments would he have to make?
5 At the end of the story, where do your sympathies lie? With Pyecraft? With Formalyn?

Writing

1 Pyecraft's problem came about because he asked for a way to reduce his weight. Imagine a similar problem (for example, someone who wants to be taller, shorter, more intelligent, stronger, wealthier) and write a story that has a structure like this one. You could also look at other stories that pursue a similar theme—perhaps the best known being the Greek legend of King Midas.
2 Formalyn suggests to Pyecraft that there may be advantages in his condition (for example, in a shipwreck). Write a story in which Pyecraft's weightlessness helps him out of some difficulty—at least temporarily.

Notes

page 126   *space:* a short period of time
a priori: literally, "from first principles"; a phrase used to describe deductive thinking (from general statements or principles to particular instances).
gormandised: from the French word *gourmand,* a lover of fine food, it came to mean overindulgence, gluttony. Perhaps Pyecraft here is ogling Formalyn's food.
Pharmacopœia: nowadays a book, usually published by an authority, containing a list of drugs with directions for their preparation and identification.

page 128   *Hindustani:* a name formerly given to the language of northern India; now known as Hindi.

page 129   *Was the egg addled?:* a stale or rotten egg.
pariah dog: an Indian term for a stray dog (a pariah is an outcast).

page 130 *Bloomsbury:* a suburb of London.

Trappistine: a liqueur made by the Trappist monks (c.f. Benedictine; Chartreuse)

vittles: food—a corruption of "victuals".

sooit: a corruption of "suet"—solid fat from around the loins and kidneys of certain animals, used in cooking.

page 132 *Santos-Dumont:* pioneer aviator, credited with perfecting the first monoplane.

page 133 *poetical justice:* an ideal justice that poets are said to exercise; the idea that a person "gets what they deserve".

page 134 *niente:* Italian for "nothing".

nefas: Latin—a sin or a crime; shocking or dreadful. It doesn't seem to make sense in this context.

Oscar Wilde
The Happy Prince

Oscar Wilde (1856-1900) was born in Dublin, Ireland. His best known works are his plays, especially *The Importance of Being Earnest.* "The Happy Prince" was first published in 1888. It was one of a number of stories he wrote originally for his son. He spent two years in prison after a much celebrated and controversial court case which eventually resulted in his conviction on a homosexuality charge (1895). He left England soon after his release and died in France. He is still regarded as one of the greatest wits in the English language.

Wilde calls this story a fairy tale. *The Oxford Companion to Children's Literature* defines fairy tales as "narratives, set in the distant past, of events that would be impossible in the real world. They often include magical happenings and the appearance of fairies, but the supernatural does not always feature in them, and the heroes and heroines are usually mortal people. Such creatures as giants, dwarfs, witches and ogres frequently play a part, as well as talking animals."

HIGH above the city, on a tall column, stood the statue of the Happy Prince. He was gilded all over with thin leaves of fine gold, for eyes he had two bright sapphires, and a large red ruby glowed on his sword hilt.

He was very much admired indeed. "He is as beautiful as a weathercock," remarked one of the Town Councillors who wished to gain a reputation for having artistic tastes; "only not quite so useful," he added, fearing lest people should think him unpractical, which he really was not.

"Why can't you be like the Happy Prince?" asked a sensible mother of her little boy who was crying for the moon. "The Happy Prince never dreams of crying for anything."

"I am glad there is someone in the world who is quite happy," muttered a disappointed man as he gazed at the wonderful statue.

"He looks just like an angel," said the Charity Children as they came out of the cathedral in their bright scarlet cloaks and their clean white pinafores.

"How do you know?" said the Mathematical Master, "you have never seen one."

"Ah! but we have, in our dreams," answered the children; and the Mathematical Master frowned and looked very severe, for he did not approve of children dreaming.

One night there flew over the city a little Swallow. His friends had gone away to Egypt six weeks before, but he had stayed behind, for he was in love with the most beautiful Reed. He had met her early in the spring as he was flying down the river after a big yellow moth, and had been so attracted by her slender waist that he had stopped to talk to her.

"Shall I love you?" said the Swallow, who liked to come to the point at once, and the Reed made him a low bow. So he flew round and round her, touching the water with his wings, and making silver ripples. This was his courtship, and it lasted all through the summer.

"It is a ridiculous attachment," twittered the other Swallows; "she has no money, and far too many relations"; and indeed the river was quite full of Reeds. Then, when the autumn came they all flew away.

After they had gone he felt lonely, and began to tire of his lady-love. "She has no conversation," he said, "and I am afraid that she is a coquette, for she is always flirting with the wind." And certainly, whenever the wind blew, the Reed made the most graceful curtsies. "I admit that she is domestic," he continued, "but I love travelling, and my wife, consequently, should love travelling also."

"Will you come away with me?" he said finally to her, but the Reed shook her head, she was so attached to her home.

"You have been trifling with me," he cried. "I am off to the Pyramids. Good-bye!" and he flew away.

All day long he flew, and at night-time he arrived at the city. "Where shall I put up?" he said; "I hope the town has made preparations."

Then he saw the statue on the tall column.

"I will put up there," he cried; "it is a fine position, with plenty of fresh air." So he alighted just between the feet of the Happy Prince.

"I have a golden bedroom," he said softly to himself as he looked round, and he prepared to go to sleep; but just as he was putting his head under his wing a large drop of water fell on him. "What a curious thing!" he cried; "there is not a single cloud in the sky, the stars are quite clear and bright, and yet it was raining. The climate in the north of Europe is really dreadful. The Reed used to like the rain, but that was merely her selfishness."

Then another drop fell.

"What is the use of a statue if it cannot keep the rain off?" he said; "I must look for a good chimney-pot," and he determined to fly away.

But before he had opened his wings, a third drop fell, and he looked up and saw—Ah! what did he see?

The eyes of the Happy Prince were filled with tears, and tears were running down his golden cheeks. His face was so beautiful in the moonlight that the little Swallow was filled with pity.

"Who are you?" he said.

"I am the Happy Prince."

"Why are you weeping then?" asked the Swallow; "you have quite drenched me."

"When I was alive and had a human heart," answered the statue, "I did not know what tears were, for I lived in the Palace of Sans-Souci, where sorrow is not allowed to enter. In the daytime I played with my companions in the garden, and in the evening I led the dance in the Great Hall. Round the garden ran a very lofty wall, but I never cared to ask what lay beyond it, everything about me was so beautiful. My courtiers called me the Happy Prince, and happy indeed I was, if pleasure be happiness. So I lived, and so I died. And now that I am dead they have set me up here so high that I can see all the ugliness and all the misery of my city, and though my heart is made of lead yet I cannot choose but weep."

"What! is he not solid gold?" said the Swallow to himself. He was too polite to make any personal remarks out loud.

"Far away," continued the statue in a low musical voice, "far away in a little street there is a poor house. One of the windows is open, and through it I can see a woman seated at a table. Her face is thin and worn, and she has coarse, red hands, all pricked by the needle, for she is a seamstress. She is embroidering passion-flowers on a satin gown for the loveliest of the Queen's maids-of-honour to wear at the next Court ball. In a bed in the corner of the room her little boy is lying ill. He has a fever, and is asking for oranges. His mother has nothing to give him but river water, so he is crying. Swallow, Swallow, little Swallow, will you not bring her the ruby out of my sword-hilt? My feet are fastened to this pedestal and I cannot move."

"I am waited for in Egypt," said the Swallow. "My friends are flying up and down the Nile, and talking to the large lotus-flowers. Soon they will go to sleep in the tomb of the great King. The King is there himself in his painted coffin. He is wrapped in yellow linen, and embalmed with spices. Round his neck is a chain of pale green jade, and his hands are like withered leaves."

"Swallow, Swallow, little Swallow," said the Prince, "will you not stay with me for one night, and be my messenger? The boy is so thirsty, and the mother so sad."

"I don't think I like boys," answered the Swallow. "Last summer, when I was staying on the river, there were two rude boys, the miller's sons, who were always throwing stones at me. They never hit me, of course; we swallows fly far too well for that, and besides I come of a family famous for its agility; but still, it was a mark of disrespect."

But the Happy Prince looked so sad that the little Swallow was sorry. "It is very cold here," he said; "but I will stay with you for one night, and be your messenger."

"Thank you, little Swallow," said the Prince.

So the Swallow picked out the great ruby from the Prince's sword, and flew away with it in his beak over the roofs of the town.

He passed by the cathedral tower, where the white marble angels were sculptured. He passed by the palace and heard the sound of dancing. A beautiful girl came out on the balcony with her lover. "How wonderful the stars are," he said to her, "and how wonderful is the power of love!"

"I hope my dress will be ready in time for the State ball," she answered; "I have ordered passion-flowers to be embroidered on it: but the seamstresses are so lazy."

He passed over the river, and saw the lanterns hanging to the masts of the ships. He passed over the Ghetto, and saw the old Jews bargaining with each other, and weighing out money in copper scales. At last he came to the poor house and looked in. The boy was tossing feverishly on his bed, and the mother had fallen asleep, she was so tired. In he hopped, and laid the great ruby on the table beside the woman's thimble. Then he flew gently round the bed, fanning the boy's forehead with his wings. "How cool I feel!" said the boy, "I must be getting better;" and he sank into a delicious slumber.

Then the Swallow flew back to the Happy Prince, and told him what he had done. "It is curious," he remarked, "but I feel quite warm now, although it is so cold."

"That is because you have done a good action," said the Prince. And the little Swallow began to think, and then he fell asleep. Thinking always made him sleepy.

When day broke he flew down to the river and had a bath."What a remarkable phenomenon!" said the Professor of Ornithology as he was passing over the bridge. "A swallow in winter!" And he wrote a long letter about it to the local newspaper. Everyone quoted it, it was full of so many words that they could not understand.

"Tonight I go to Egypt," said the Swallow, and he was in high spirits at the prospect. He visited all the public monuments, and sat a long time on top of the church steeple. Wherever he went the Sparrows chirruped, and said to each other, "What a distinguished stranger!" so he enjoyed himself very much.

When the moon rose he flew back to the Happy Prince. "Have you any commissions for Egypt?" he cried; "I am just starting."

"Swallow, Swallow, little Swallow," said the Prince, "will you not stay with me one night longer?"

"I am waited for in Egypt," answered the Swallow. "Tomorrow my friends will fly up to the Second Cataract. The river-horse couches there among the bulrushes, and on a great granite throne sits the God Memnon. All night long he watches the stars, and when the morning star shines he utters one cry of joy, and then he is silent. At noon the yellow lions come down to the water's edge to drink. They have eyes like green beryls, and their roar is louder than the roar of the cataract."

"Swallow, Swallow, little Swallow," said the Prince, "far away across the city I see a young man in a garret. He is leaning over a desk covered with papers, and in a tumbler by his side there is a bunch of withered violets. His hair is brown and crisp, and his lips are red as a pomegranate, and he has large and dreamy eyes. He is trying to finish a play for the Director of the Theatre, but he is too cold to write any more. There is no fire in the grate, and hunger has made him faint."

"I will wait with you one night longer," said the Swallow, who really had a good heart. "Shall I take him another ruby?"

"Alas! I have no ruby now," said the Prince: "my eyes are all that I have left. They are made of rare sapphires, which were brought out of India a thousand years ago. Pluck out one of them and take it to him. He will sell it to the jeweller, and buy firewood, and finish his play."

"Dear Prince," said the Swallow, "I cannot do that;" and he began to weep.

"Swallow, Swallow, little Swallow," said the Prince, "do as I command you."

So the Swallow plucked out the Prince's eye, and flew away to the student's garret. It was easy enough to get in, as there was a hole in the roof. Through this he darted, and came into the room. The young man had his head buried in his hands, so he did not hear the flutter of the bird's wings, and when he looked up he found the beautiful sapphire lying on the withered violets.

"I am beginning to be appreciated," he cried; "this is from some great admirer. Now I can finish my play," and he looked quite happy.

The next day the Swallow flew down to the harbour. He sat on the mast of a large vessel and watched the sailors hauling big chests out of the hold with ropes. "Heave a-hoy!" they shouted as each chest came up. "I am going to Egypt!" cried the Swallow, but nobody minded, and when the moon rose he flew back to the Happy Prince.

"I am come to bid you good-bye," he cried.

"Swallow, Swallow, little Swallow," said the Prince, "will you not stay with me one night longer?"

"It is winter," answered the Swallow, "and the chill snow will soon be here. In Egypt the sun is warm on the green palm-trees, and the crocodiles lie in the mud and look lazily about them. My companions are building a nest in the Temple of Baalbek, and the pink and white doves are watching them, and cooing to each other. Dear Prince, I must leave you, but I will never forget you, and next spring I will bring you back two beautiful jewels in place of those you have given away. The ruby shall be redder than a red rose, and the sapphire shall be as blue as the great sea."

"In the square below," said the Happy Prince, "there stands a little match-girl. She has let her matches fall in the gutter, and they are all spoiled. Her father will beat her if she does not bring home some money, and she is crying. She has no shoes or stockings, and her little head is bare. Pluck out my other eye, and give it to her, and her father will not beat her."

"I will stay with you one night longer," said the Swallow, "but I cannot pluck out your eye. You would be quite blind then."

"Swallow, Swallow, little Swallow," said the Prince, "do as I command you."

So he plucked out the Prince's other eye, and darted down with it. He swooped past the match-girl, and slipped the jewel into the palm of her hand. "What a lovely bit of glass!" cried the little girl; and she ran home, laughing.

Then the Swallow came back to the Prince. "You are blind now," he said, "so I will stay with you always."

"No, little Swallow," said the poor Prince, "you must go away to Egypt."

"I will stay with you always," said the Swallow, and he slept at the Prince's feet.

All the next day he sat on the Prince's shoulder, and told him stories of what he had seen in strange lands. He told him of the red ibises, who stand in long rows on the banks of the Nile, and catch goldfish in their beaks; of the Sphinx, who is as old as the world itself, and lives in the desert, and knows everything; of the merchants, who walk slowly by the side of their camels and carry amber beads in their hands; of the King of the Mountains of the Moon, who is as black as ebony, and worships a large crystal; of the great green snake that sleeps in a palm-tree, and has twenty priests to feed it with honey-cakes; and of the pygmies who sail over a big lake on large flat leaves, and are always at war with the butterflies.

"Dear little Swallow," said the Prince, "you tell me of marvellous things, but more marvellous than anything is the suffering of men and of women. There is no Mystery so great as Misery. Fly over my city, little Swallow, and tell me what you see there."

So the Swallow flew over the great city, and saw the rich making merry in their beautiful houses, while the beggars were sitting at the gates. He flew into dark lanes, and saw the white faces of starving children looking out listlessly at the black streets. Under the archway of a bridge two little boys were lying in one another's arms to try and keep themselves warm. "How hungry we are!" they said. "You must not lie here," shouted the watchman, and they wandered out into the rain.

Then he flew back and told the Prince what he had seen.

"I am covered with fine gold," said the Prince, "you must take it off, leaf by leaf, and give it to my poor; the living always think that gold can make them happy."

Leaf after leaf of the fine gold the Swallow picked off, till the Happy Prince looked quite dull and grey. Leaf after leaf of the fine gold he brought to the poor, and the children's faces grew rosier, and they laughed and played games in the street. "We have bread now!" they cried.

Then the snow came, and after the snow came the frost. The streets looked as if they were made of silver, they were so bright and glistening; long icicles like crystal daggers hung down from the eaves of the houses, everybody went about in furs, and the little boys wore scarlet caps and skated on the ice.

The poor little Swallow grew colder and colder, but he would not leave the Prince, he loved him too well. He picked up crumbs outside the baker's door when the baker was not looking, and tried to keep himself warm by flapping his wings.

But at last he knew that he was going to die. He had just enough strength to fly up to the Prince's shoulder once more. "Good-bye, dear Prince!" he murmured, "will you let me kiss your hand?"

"I am glad that you are going to Egypt at last, little Swallow," said the Prince, "you have stayed too long here; but you must kiss me on the lips, for I love you."

"It is not to Egypt that I am going," said the Swallow. "I am going to the House of Death. Death is the brother of Sleep, is he not?"

And he kissed the Happy Prince on the lips, and fell down dead at his feet.

At that moment a curious crack sounded inside the statue, as if something has broken. The fact is that the leaden heart had snapped right in two. It certainly was a dreadfully hard frost.

Early the next morning the Mayor was walking in the square below in company with the Town Councillors. As they passed the column he looked up at the statue: "Dear me! how shabby the Happy Prince looks!" he said.

"How shabby, indeed!" cried the Town Councillors, who always agreed with the Mayor: and they went up to look at it.

"The ruby has fallen out of his sword, his eyes are gone, and he is golden no longer," said the Mayor; "in fact, he is little better than a beggar!"

"Little better than a beggar," said the Town Councillors.

"And here is actually a dead bird at his feet!" continued the Mayor. "We must really issue a proclamation that birds are not to be allowed to die here." And the Town Clerk made a note of the suggestion.

So they pulled down the statue of the Happy Prince. "As he is no longer beautiful he is no longer useful," said the Art Professor at the University.

Then they melted the statue in a furnace, and the Major held a meeting of the Corporation to decide what was to be done with the metal. "We must have another statue, of course," he said, "and it shall be a statue of myself."

"Of myself," said each of the Town Councillors, and they quarrelled. When I last heard of them they were quarrelling still.

"What a strange thing!" said the overseer of the workmen at the foundry. "This broken lead heart will not melt in the furnace. We must throw it away." So they threw it on a dust-heap where the dead Swallow was also lying.

"Bring me the two most precious things in the city," said God to one of His Angels; and the Angel brought Him the leaden heart and the dead bird.

"You have rightly chosen," said God, "for in my garden of Paradise this little bird shall sing for evermore, and in my city of gold the Happy Prince shall praise me."

❖

Questions

1 What is it that makes "The Happy Prince" a fairy tale? Compare it with other fairy tales you know (like "Cinderella", "Goldilocks and the Three Bears", "Rumpelstiltskin" or "The Ugly Duckling").
2 "Fairy tales are written for children, but 'The Happy Prince' will appeal to people of all ages."

Do you agree? Give reasons for your answer, and refer to particular incidents or statements. Some statements you could begin with are:

- *. . . the Mathematical Master frowned and looked very severe, for he did not approve of children dreaming.* (page 138)
- *The eyes of the Happy Prince were filled with tears, and tears were running down his golden cheeks. His face was so beautiful in the moonlight that the little Swallow was filled with pity.* (page 140)
- *'What a remarkable phenomenon!' said the Professor of Ornithology as he was passing over the bridge. 'A swallow in winter!' And he wrote a long letter about it to the local newspaper. Everyone quoted it, it was full of so many words that they could not understand.* (page 141)
- *All the next day he sat on the Prince's shoulder, and told him stories of what he had seen in strange lands. He told him of the red ibises, who stand in long rows on the banks of the Nile, and catch goldfish in their beaks; of the Sphinx, who is as old as the world itself, and lives in the desert and knows everything . . .* (page 143)
- *'And here is actually a dead bird at his feet!' continued the Mayor. 'We must really issue a proclamation that birds are not to be allowed to die here.' And the Town Clerk made a note of the suggestion.* (page 145)

Writing

1 *. . . 'Bring me the two most precious things in the city' . . .*
   Write a story based upon this request (either a fairy story or a tale set in modern times).
2 Keeping in mind the characteristics of fairy tales mentioned on page 137, write your own fairy story. Try to present a draft of the story to a young audience, and ask them to comment on its strengths and weaknesses before writing a final draft. Consider also the best way to present your story—for example, a tape with sound effects, or a book with illustrations.

Notes

page 137   *crying for the moon:* an expression meaning wanting what cannot be had; expecting too much.
   Charity Children: children in an orphanage reliant on either church or public charity.
page 138   *a coquette:* a flirt.

page 140   *Sans-Souci:* French for "without care". The name of the summer palace of Frederick the Great of Prussia.

page 142   *Second Cataract:* There are six cataracts (rapids) on the Nile in present-day Sudan and southern Egypt. The second cataract would have been near the boundary of ancient Egypt.

the God Memnon: mythological king of Ethiopia. The colossal statue at Thebes in ancient Egypt was called the statue of Memnon.

page 143   *the Temple of Baalbek:* an ancient city in what is now Lebanon.

Appendix

The Drover's Wife

This version of Henry Lawson's story is from *The Victorian Readers Fifth Book* (second edition, 1940).

THE two-roomed house is built of round timber, slabs, and stringy-bark, and floored with split slabs. A big, bark kitchen standing at one end is larger than the house itself, verandah included.

Bush all round—bush with no horizon, for the country is flat. No ranges in the distance. The bush consists of stunted, rotten, native apple-trees. No undergrowth. Nothing to relieve the eye save the darker green of a few sheoaks which are sighing above the narrow, almost waterless, creek. Nineteen miles to the nearest house.

The drover, an ex-squatter, is away with sheep. His wife and children are left here alone.

Four ragged, dried-up-looking children are playing about the house. Suddenly, one of them yells, "Snake! Mother, here's a snake!"

The gaunt, sun-browned bushwoman dashes from the kitchen, snatches her baby from the ground, holds it on her left hip, and reaches for a stick.

"Where is it?"

"Here! Gone into the wood-heap!" yells the eldest boy—a sharp-faced, excited urchin of eleven. "Stop there, mother! I'll have him. Stand back! I'll have him!"

"Tommy, come here, or you'll be bitten. Come here at once when I tell you!"

The youngster comes reluctantly, carrying a stick bigger than himself. Then he yells triumphantly, "There it goes—under the house!" and darts away with club uplifted. At the same time, the big, black, yellow-eyed dog-of-all-breeds, who has shown the wildest interest in the proceedings, breaks his chain, and rushes after the snake. He is a moment late, however, and his nose reaches the crack in the slabs just as the end of its tail disappears. Almost at the same moment, the boy's club comes down and skins the aforesaid nose. Alligator takes small notice

148

of this, and proceeds to undermine the building; but he is subdued, after a struggle, and chained up. They cannot afford to lose him.

The drover's wife makes the children stand together near the dog-house while she watches for the snake. She gets two small dishes of milk, and sets them down near the wall to tempt it to come out; but an hour goes by, and it does not show itself.

It is near sunset, and a thunder-storm is coming. The children must be brought inside. She will not take them into the house, for she knows the snake is there, and may, at any moment, come up through the cracks in the rough, slab floor; so she carries several armfuls of firewood into the kitchen, and then takes the children there. The kitchen has no floor, or, rather, an earthen one—called a "ground floor" in this part of the bush. There is a large, roughly made table in the centre of the place. She brings the children in, and makes them get on this table. They are two boys and two girls—mere babies. She gives them some supper, and then, before it gets dark, she goes into the house and snatches up some pillows and bed-clothes—expecting to see or lay her hand on the snake at any minute. She makes a bed on the kitchen table for the children, and sits down beside it to watch all night.

She had an eye on the corner and a green sapling club laid in readiness on the dresser by her side; also her sewing basket and a copy of *The Young Ladies' Journal*. She has brought the dog into the room.

Tommy turns in under protest, but says he'll lie awake all night and smash that snake; he has his club with him under the bed-clothes.

Near midnight. The children are all asleep, and she sits there still, sewing and reading by turns. From time to time she glances round the floor and wall-plate, and whenever she hears a noise she reaches for the stick. The thunder-storm comes on, and the wind, rushing through the cracks in the slab wall, threatens to blow out her candle. She places it on a sheltered part of the dresser, and fixes up a newspaper to protect it. At every flash of lightning, the cracks between the slabs gleam like polished silver. The thunder rolls, and the rain comes down in torrents.

Alligator lies at full length on the floor, with his eyes turned towards the partition. She knows, by this, that the snake is there. There are large cracks in that wall, opening under the floor of the dwelling-house.

She is not a coward, but recent events have shattered her nerves. A little son of her brother-in-law was lately bitten by a snake, and died. Besides, she has not heard from her husband for six months, and is anxious about him.

He was a drover, and started squatting here when they were married. The drought ruined him. He had to sacrifice the remnant of his flock and go droving again. He intends to move his family into the nearest town when he comes back; and in the meantime his brother, who lives along the main road, comes over about once a month with provisions. The wife has still a couple of cows, one horse, and a few sheep. The brother-in-law kills one of the latter occasionally, gives her what she needs of it, and takes the rest in return for other provisions.

It must be near one or two o'clock. The fire is burning low. Alligator lies with his head resting on his paws, and watches the wall. He is not a very beautiful dog to look at, and the light shows numerous old wounds where the hair will not grow. He is afraid of nothing on the face of the earth or under it. He will tackle a bullock as readily as he will tackle a flea. He hates all other dogs—except kangaroo-dogs—and has a marked dislike to friends or relations of the family. They seldom call, however. He sometimes makes friends with strangers. He hates snakes, and has killed many, but he will be bitten some day and die; most snake-dogs end that way.

Now and then the bushwoman lays down her work and watches, and listens, and thinks. She has few pleasures to think of as she sits here alone by the fire, on guard against a snake. All days are much the same to her; but on Sunday afternoons she dresses herself, tidies the children, smartens up baby, and goes for a lonely walk along the bush-track, pushing an old perambulator in front of her. She does this every Sunday. She takes as much care to make herself and the children look smart as she would if she were going to "do the block" in the city. There is nothing to see, however, and not a soul to meet. You might walk for twenty miles along this track without being able to fix a point in your mind, unless you are a bushman.

It must be near daylight now. The room is very close and hot because of the fire. Alligator still watches the wall from time to time. Suddenly he becomes greatly interested; he draws himself a few inches nearer the partition, and a thrill runs through his body. The hair on the back of his neck begins to bristle, and the battle-light is in his yellow eyes. She knows what this means, and lays her hand on the stick. The lower end of one of the partition slabs has a large crack on both sides. An evil pair of small, bright, bead-like eyes glisten at one of these holes. The snake—a black one—comes slowly out, about a foot, and moves its head up and down. The dog lies still, and the woman sits as one fascinated.

The snake comes out a foot farther. She lifts her stick, and the reptile, as though suddenly aware of danger, sticks his head in through the crack on the other side of the slab, and hurries to get his tail round after him. Alligator springs, and his jaws come together with a snap. He misses this time, for his nose is large and the snake's body close down in the angle formed by the slabs and the floor. He snaps again as the tail comes round. He has the snake now, and tugs it out eighteen inches. Thud, thud, comes the woman's club on the ground. Alligator pulls again. Thud, thud. Alligator pulls some more. He has the snake out now—a black brute, five feet long. The head rises to dart about, but the dog has the enemy close to the neck. He is a big, heavy dog, but quick as a terrier. The eldest boy wakes up, seizes his stick, and tries to get out of bed; but his mother forces him back with a grip of iron. Thud, thud—the snake's back is broken in several places. Thud, thud—its head is crushed, and Alligator's nose skinned again.

She lifts the mangled reptile on the point of her stick, carries it to the fire, and throws it in; then piles on the wood, and watches the snake burn. The boy and the dog watch too. She lays her hand on the dog's head, and all the fierce, angry light dies out of his yellow eyes. The younger children are quieted, and presently go to sleep. The boy stands for a moment in his shirt, watching the fire. Presently he looks up to her, sees the tears in her eyes, and, throwing his arms round her neck, exclaims: "Mother, I'll never go droving."

And she hugs him to her breast, and kisses him; and they sit thus together while the sickly daylight breaks over the bush.

HENRY LAWSON.

Acknowledgements

The authors and publishers are grateful to the following for permission to reproduce copyright material:

Chatto & Windus/The Hogarth Press and the William Faulkner Estate for "The Liar" by William Faulkner from *New Orleans Sketches*; Harper and Brothers for "The Secret Life of Walter Mitty" by James Thurber; Jonathan Cape Ltd on behalf of the Executors of the James Joyce Estate for "Eveline" by James Joyce; The Society of Authors as the literary representative of the Estate of W. W. Jacobs for "The Monkey's Paw".

While every care has been taken to trace and acknowledge copyright, the publishers tender their apologies for any accidental infringement where copyright has proved untraceable. They would be pleased to come to a suitable arrangement with the rightful owner in each case.